The Case of the Graceful Goldens

A Thousand Islands Doggy Inn Mystery

B.R. Snow

Copyright © 2017 B.R. Snow
ISBN: 978-1-942691-23-5

Website: www.brsnow.net/
Twitter: @BernSnow
Facebook: facebook.com/bernsnow

Cover Design: Reggie Cullen
Cover Photo: James R. Miller

Other Books by B.R. Snow

The Thousand Islands Doggy Inn Mysteries

- The Case of the Abandoned Aussie
- The Case of the Brokenhearted Bulldog
- The Case of the Caged Cockers
- The Case of the Dapper Dandie Dinmont
- The Case of the Eccentric Elkhound
- The Case of the Faithful Frenchie

The Whiskey Run Chronicles

- Episode 1 – The Dry Season Approaches
- Episode 2 – Friends and Enemies
- Episode 3 – Let the Games Begin
- Episode 4 – Enter the Revenuer
- Episode 5 – A Changing Landscape
- Episode 6 – Entrepreneurial Spirits
- Episode 7 – All Hands On Deck

The Damaged Posse

- American Midnight
- Larrikin Gene
- Sneaker World
- Summerman
- The Duplicates

Other Books

- Divorce Hotel
- Either Ore

To Stella

Chapter 1

It was sunny but cold, and while I knew that the early morning frost would soon melt, the overnight temperature that had dropped into the teens was a stark reminder that winter was on the way. The ground had been *crunchy* when I took Chloe and Captain out to do their business an hour earlier, and now from the comfort of the living room, I could tell that Chef Claire was also dealing with a noisy morning walk as she carefully made her way across the slippery lawn. Al and Dente, her two Golden Retrievers, seemed less concerned with the cold and wind and wanted to play instead of focusing on the task at hand. Chef Claire grudgingly agreed and spent the next few minutes throwing tennis balls and then struggling to get them out of her dog's mouths.

Josie approached and stood next to me sipping coffee as we stared out the picture window overlooking the section of lawn that led down to our dock.

"They're such gorgeous dogs."

"They certainly are," I said. "And she's doing a great job with them."

Chef Claire had been given both dogs when they were eight weeks old for her birthday. Jackson, our former chief of police, and Freddie, our local medical examiner, had each given her a

1

puppy completely unaware what the other's gift was. The puppies were from the same litter, and Chef Claire had been overwhelmed by their generosity. Both men were still holding out hope that she would eventually profess her undying love and hoped that the gift of a puppy might tilt the scales in their favor. But despite the home run they had hit with the puppies, Jackson and Freddie remained firmly in Chef Claire's category of *just good friends.*

I watched Chef Claire hug herself as she bounced on her toes and fought the strong north wind. She waited, then watched both dogs complete their morning mission, and turned to head back toward the house. She waited for the dogs to follow her, but Al and Dente sat down and stared at her, their heads cocked, obviously waiting for a reward.

"Watch this," I said to Josie.

Chef Claire trudged toward the swing that hung from a tree at the edge of the lawn and patted the high-backed wooden seat. We'd made the swing out of an old glider that used to sit on our verandah, but rarely used it. But the two Goldens had discovered it an early age, and any thoughts we had about removing the swing had disappeared. Al and Dente dashed across the lawn and leaped up on the seat, then turned and sat down facing the house. The dogs stuck the landing, and the swing barely moved.

"Graceful," Josie said, finishing her coffee.

"That's the word," I said, marveling at the dogs' agility.

Chef Claire began pushing the swing, and the dogs' tongues lolled. As they swung back and forth, they seemed to have a huge smile on their faces. But there was no wondering about the smile on Chef Claire's face: She was beaming. A few minutes later Chef Claire made her way back to the house with Al and Dente leading the way. The dogs trotted into the living room and began rolling around on the floor with Captain and Chloe. Chef Claire tossed her coat over a chair, sat down on a couch and smiled at all four dogs.

"How on earth did you teach them to jump up on the swing?" Josie said.

"I really didn't," Chef Claire said. "A couple of weeks ago I just tried patting the seat with my hand. And they figured it out right away. Now, I can't get them off it."

"Smart," Josie said, looking down at the two Goldens now draped across Chef Claire's feet. "Aren't you, Dente?"

The female popped to her feet, sat on her haunches, and placed her front paws on Josie's knees. Josie rubbed Dente's head and glanced at the male, Al, who was returning her stare.

"You too, Al. He's a good boy. Aren't you Al?" Josie said.

Al stared at Josie, then nuzzled Chef Claire's foot.

"I can't believe it," Josie said. "He's still mad at me. How is that possible?"

Several weeks ago, Josie had neutered and spayed the dogs. Dente hadn't harbored any resentment toward Josie, but Al still hadn't forgiven her and remained aloof. Unaccustomed to receiving anything but unconditional love from every dog she came in contact with, Josie was perplexed by the dog's ongoing indifference to her.

"He'll come around," Chef Claire said, laughing.

"I'm beginning to wonder," Josie said, leaning down to rub Al's head. "I've never seen a dog hold a grudge this long."

"Well, you did say he was a very smart dog," I deadpanned. "Maybe he's also a really good judge of character."

"Funny," Josie said, settling back into the couch.

"Oh, I almost forgot," I said, heading for the armoire.

I removed four identical boxes and gave one to Josie and two to Chef Claire. I kept the fourth one for myself.

"Early Christmas present," I said, opening my box.

"A GPS tracker?" Josie said.

"Yeah. Apparently, the latest and greatest in dog security," I said, removing the small object. "It attaches to the dog's collar and has a signal with a radius of five miles. Just in case any of these guys ever happened to get loose."

"Like any of these guys would ever have a reason to go anywhere," Josie said, laughing.

I looked at the two Goldens draped over Chef Claire's feet, then glanced over at Chloe, my Australian Shepherd who was sleeping in front of the fire and tucked under one of Captain's front paws. Josie's Newfie was stretched out full-length and snoring contentedly.

"You've got a point there," I said, laughing. "But I told the sales rep we'd give them a try for a month and let him know what we thought. There's an app you can download to keep track of your dog right from your phone."

"So it just snaps around the collar?" Chef Claire said.

"Yeah. Just try to keep Al from getting it off and eating it," I said.

"And try to keep him out of my closet," Josie said, glaring down at Al. "He chewed another pair of my shoes yesterday."

"I told you I'd reimburse you for those," Chef Claire said.

"Don't worry about it," Josie said. "It's not the money. And I shouldn't have left the closet door open."

"It's really strange," Chef Claire said. "He hasn't chewed anything of mine in a couple months."

"I just told you," Josie said. "He's still mad at me. Aren't you, Al?"

Al glanced up at Josie, then closed his eyes and rolled over.

"What a good boy," I said, laughing. "Since we're going to be in Grand Cayman for a week, I thought it might give us a little extra peace of mind knowing they're wearing these."

"Sammy and Jill will keep a close eye on them," Josie said.

Sammy and Jill were our two lead staff members, and, in addition to running things at the Inn while we were away, would be housesitting.

"I guess it can't hurt," Josie said. "Captain. Come here, boy."

The Newfie woke, stretched, then walked over to Josie and stood patiently while she attached the device to his collar. Then

Josie removed her phone, downloaded the app, and nodded her head.

"How about that?" she said. "That was easy. And the tracker is working great. In case you weren't sure, at the moment Captain is one foot away from me."

At one hundred and twenty pounds and still growing, the Newfie was a bit hard to miss.

"Wow. That was easy," Chef Claire said, examining both of the dogs' collars and checking the signal on her phone. "Thanks, Suzy."

"No problem. Hopefully, we won't ever need them," I said, attaching the tracking device to Chloe's collar.

"I need to run to town," Chef Claire said. "Do you mind if I borrow your SUV?"

"It's a bit of a mess at the moment," I said.

"How can you tell?" Josie deadpanned.

"Funny. The front console that Rooster fixed a couple months ago has broken loose again. And there's a new hole in the floor behind the driver seat. It looks like it completely rusted through."

Chef Claire and Josie shared an amused glance.

"Don't start," I said. "I'm going to get a new car."

"When?" Josie said.

"As soon as we get back from vacation," I said.

"I need to go to the store and pick up my bread order," Chef Claire said. "And there's no way I can fit it all in my car."

"Let's take the boat," I said. "The sun's out so it shouldn't be too bad out there."

We'd left the boat in the water longer than any other previous year. The fall had been mild, and the River was still devoid of ice. As such, we'd been able to get in several more boat rides than we did most other years.

"You want to come along?" Chef Claire said.

"Sure. I haven't seen Jackson all week, and you'll need a hand carrying all that bread. What do you say, Chloe?"

"Chloe says no," Josie said. "Today is booster shot day. Rabies, Lyme, Leptospirosis, and Coronavirus."

"I forgot," I said. "Sorry, girl. But I'm sure that Al and Dente are up for a boat ride."

The Goldens perked up and cocked their heads at the mention of the boat ride. I laughed, then grabbed my coat and the keys to the boat, and we headed for the dock with the dogs leading the way. They sat on the dock and waited for us to remove the boat cover then they hopped into the boat and up onto the padded seat that ran the length of the transom. They sat side by side and stared at us.

"They're like athletes," I said, again marveling at the dogs' effortless agility.

"I know," Chef Claire said, climbing into the boat. "If they had thumbs, I'd put them to work in the restaurant."

I backed the boat out of its slip, and we made the short drive to town in less than ten minutes. I had my choice of parking spots at the town dock, and the dogs made the short jump from the boat to the dock and sat waiting for us. Chef Claire attached their leads and handed me Al's. We strolled up the empty street before making the right turn that would take us to Jackson's store.

"My mother used to send me to the store for bread when I was a kid," I said.

"Are you taking a trip down memory lane?" Chef Claire said.

"Yeah, I guess I am. It's funny what triggers childhood memories. A couple times a week I'd take my dog and we'd walk to the store for milk and bread."

"I bet your mom never sent you out for a hundred loaves," Chef Claire said.

"No, this is a first."

Chapter 2

We walked across the parking lot and stopped outside the store under an alcove that was shielded from the wind. Chef Claire pulled about twenty feet of cord from the retractable leashes and secured them to a post Jackson had recently installed. She knelt down in front of Al and Dente and spoke to them in a soft voice as she rubbed their heads.

"Sorry, guys," she said. "But I can't bring you in the store, so you're going to have to hang out here for a few minutes. I'll be right back."

Chef Claire stood up, and we headed for the entrance but stopped when we heard a quick blast from a car horn. We both turned around and saw the woman in an SUV waving at us. The vehicle was in a lot better shape than mine, to say the least. The driver side window went down and a gray-haired woman who was probably somewhere in her fifties beamed at us and pointed a finger at Al and Dente.

"I'd recognize those two anywhere," the woman said, turning the SUV off. "They're mine, right?"

"I beg your pardon," Chef Claire said, staring at her.

"I'm sorry," she said. "They're not mine now, of course."

"I'm going to need a little more," Chef Claire said, laughing.

"I'm so sorry," the woman said. "I'm Alexandra Vincent. Vincent Farms."

"Oh, sure," I said. "Vincent Farms. You're the Golden breeder. Lake Placid, right?"

"Saranac Lake, actually," she said, smiling. "But close enough. They're doing great. What did you end up naming them?"

"Al and Dente," Chef Claire said, glancing at her two Goldens who seemed fixated on the back seat of the woman's vehicle.

"How clever," Alexandra said. "Let me introduce you to their parents."

She lowered the back seat window about halfway, and two heads popped through the opening.

"I'd like you to meet Lucky and Lucy," Alexandra said. "Between them, they have over a hundred Best in Shows."

"You know, I never made the connection," I said, approaching the vehicle. "You were on the cover of *It's a Dog's World* a couple of months ago with them."

"Yes," Alexandra said, reaching behind her to give both of her Goldens a quick pet. "I'm riding the coattails of their fame. I never made the connection either. When I sold Al and Dente - love the names - to your two friends, I should have put two and two together."

"I'm confused," Chef Claire said.

"Alexandra and her husband run Vincent Farms. They're the top Golden breeder in the Northeast, if not the entire country."

"Oh, we're not quite that famous," Alexandra said, obviously pleased by my compliment. "Would you mind if we said hello?"

"Of course not," Chef Claire said.

Alexandra hopped out of the SUV and opened the back door. Both dogs jumped effortlessly from the car to the street and trotted toward Al and Dente to get reacquainted. I watched the dogs nuzzle each other then looked at Alexandra who was staring at the dogs with enormous pride.

"Look at that," she said, tearing up. "I don't get a chance to see this sort of reunion very often. They all recognize each other. And they look magnificent. You're obviously doing a great job raising them."

"Thank you," Chef Claire said.

"The two gentlemen who bought them from us both said their puppy was a birthday present," she said. "You were given both dogs?"

"I was."

"What a wonderful surprise that must have been," she said, continuing to watch the dogs.

"Surprise is a word for it," Chef Claire said, laughing. "But they're certainly wonderful."

"What are you doing here, Alexandra?" I said.

"At the moment, I'm looking for something I can cook for dinner."

"No, I meant what are you doing in Clay Bay? Are you here for Thanksgiving?"

11

"Well, I will be here for Thanksgiving, but that's not *why* I'm here. I'm in town to judge the Dog Show."

"Of course," I said, nodding. "In addition to being a breeder, you're also one of the top judges in the country."

"I wouldn't go that far," she said, again pleased by the compliment. "But since my husband is traveling at the moment, and my children won't be coming home until Christmas, the thought of spending Thanksgiving by myself wasn't very appealing. And while I usually take this time of year off to enjoy the holidays, your mayor personally called and invited me to judge your show. At first, I declined, but I eventually accepted. I must say that your mayor is a difficult woman to say no to."

"Tell me about it," I said, laughing. "The mayor is my mother."

Alexandra stared into the distance deep in thought, then looked at me.

"Chandler? Of course," she said. "You're Suzy Chandler. The Thousand Islands Doggy Inn, right?"

"Guilty as charged."

"I just read an article about you and your business partner," she said, nodding. "You're doing some amazing work. My, my, what a small world."

"Indeed. You're in town all by yourself?" I said.

"I am. I know the show doesn't start until Saturday, but I haven't been up here in years so I thought I'd come in a couple of days early and get organized," she said, kneeling down to pet Al and Dente. "But I'm never alone as long as I have Lucky and Lucy with me. And I rarely go anywhere without them."

"Then you can stop worrying about cooking dinner," I said. "You're going to have dinner with us."

"Absolutely," Chef Claire said. "And you're more than welcome to have Thanksgiving dinner with us as well. As long as you don't mind eating with about a hundred other people."

"A hundred?" Alexandra said.

"Long story," I said. "We recently opened a restaurant, and we've decided to start a new annual tradition of serving Thanksgiving dinner to folks who aren't able to or aren't planning on cooking. You know, some of our elderly residents and shut-ins, primarily. But everyone is welcome."

"What a wonderful thing to do," Alexandra said.

"Actually, it was my mother's idea."

"And she is very difficult to say no to, right?"

"Indeed," I said, laughing. "But we didn't put up much of a fight. It should be fun."

"Well, count me in," Alexandra said.

"Speaking of which, there are a hundred loaves of bread inside with my name on them," Chef Claire said.

"Of course," Alexandra said. "I'll go in with you. I need to pick up a few other things."

She opened the back door of her SUV and whistled softly. Both her dogs trotted toward her and hopped effortlessly into the back seat. She closed the door, and their heads once again appeared in the opening.

"I'll be right back," she said, reaching through the open window to pet them. "You be good."

"They're beautiful dogs," I said, staring at the two Goldens.

"Yes, they are," she said, beaming at them. "And I don't know what I'd do without them."

All three of us headed inside the store, and we left Alexandra in the snack food aisle while we headed for the back of the store. We found Jackson near the loading dock. He had his back to us and was comparing several stacks of boxes and crates to an order slip he was holding.

"Four, five, six," he said, counting out loud.

"Seven, eight, eleven," I said, counting along with him.

Jackson turned and gave me a small smile.

"Funny. Hi, Chef Claire. Your bread just came in. One hundred loaves. That's a lot of stuffing. I assume that means Josie has confirmed."

Chef Claire and I both laughed.

"Are you coming to dinner?" I said.

"I wouldn't miss it," he said. "I already signed up to help out in the kitchen."

"That's great," Chef Claire said. "Thanks for doing that, Jackson."

"No problem. It'll be fun. And it'll be a nice break from counting tomatoes."

"You're mom and dad aren't coming in?" I said, doing my best to gently broach the subject of his parents' recent divorce.

Jackson frowned and sadness appeared in his eyes. Then it faded, and he shrugged.

"No, my mom is spending Thanksgiving in Spain with some ex-pats she met over there. And my dad decided to stay in Florida. He said the warm weather is agreeing with him. But I don't think he wants to deal with the memories."

"Sure, I guess I get that," I said, softly.

"Let me go get your bread," he said, wandering off.

"Divorce parents after forty years of marriage. That must be brutal to deal with," Chef Claire said.

"Yeah, I'm sure it is," I said, glancing around the loading area. "But running a grocery store this size must help keep his mind off it."

"Yeah, probably," Chef Claire said, grabbing the buzzing phone from her coat pocket. "What the heck?"

"What is it?"

"The GPS tracker just went off. Al and Dente are on the move."

"What are you talking about?" I said, breaking into a run to keep up with Chef Claire who was racing toward the front door.

We exited the store and stopped at the hitching post outside the door. Both dogs were gone, and Chef Claire looked around in all directions, wide-eyed and panicked.

15

"Al! Dente!" she called, glancing back and forth between her phone and the street. "It says they're already two miles away. How can that be?"

"What on earth is wrong?" Alexandra said, hurrying toward us. "You both flew by me inside the store."

"Al and Dente are gone," I said, glancing up and down the empty street.

"What?"

"They're almost out of range," Chef Claire said, tears streaming down her face.

"That means they're in a car," I said, reaching into my pocket for my phone. I placed the call and waited. "Chief. Suzy. No, not so good at the moment. Somebody just stole Chef Claire's dogs from in front of Jackson's place. Yeah, I know. We just put new GPS trackers on them that have five miles of coverage, and they're almost out of range. Let me ask her." I looked at Chef Claire. "What direction were they headed?"

"Southeast. That must be Route 3, right?"

"Sounds right," I said, then spoke into the phone. "Route 3. No, we didn't get a look at the vehicle. We were inside the store. Okay, yeah. We'll do that."

I ended the call and put my phone away. I looked at Chef Claire who was still staring down at her phone.

"Chief Abrams said we should head home and he'll meet us there," I said, placing a hand on her shoulder.

Chef Claire started sobbing, but nodded and began heading toward the town dock. I looked at Alexandra who was standing next to her SUV stroking her dogs' heads through the window.

"Somebody stole your dogs? Who could do something like that?" she said, tearing up.

"Someone despicable," I said. "And someone who's going to be in a world of hurt when we find them."

"If only you two could speak," she said, glancing at her dogs, then turning back to me. "Is there anything I can do?"

"I don't think so," I said. "But you should still stop by later. We usually eat around seven. I'm not sure if we'll be there, but someone will."

"Are you sure?"

"Yes," I said. "And bring Lucky and Lucy. If there's a dognapper running around, you'll want to keep a close eye on them."

"Okay. Then I'll see you this evening," Alexandra said, climbing into the driver seat.

"I sure hope so."

I waved goodbye to her and broke into a run to catch up with Chef Claire. I wasn't much of a runner, but it was the best I could do. By the time I reached the dock, Chef Claire had already started the boat and untied the lines. I clambered in, and she roared toward home before my feet landed on deck.

Chapter 3

By the time we arrived home, Chief Abrams was already in the living room and on the phone. He glanced up long enough to greet us, then refocused on the call. When he finished, he dialed another number and repeated virtually the same conversation. After about a half dozen calls, he put his phone away and gave Chef Claire a hug. She remained standing in the center of the room, shell-shocked. She'd stopped crying, but her breathing was labored and, at one point, she began hyperventilating. Josie and I did our best to calm her down and eventually managed to get her coat off. We led her to a couch, and she sat staring blankly into the fireplace.

"Well, I called local and state officials as well as the Customs and Immigration folks at the border," Chief Abrams said. "Everyone will be keeping an eye out for them. There are a lot of Golden Retrievers around, but we might have a better chance of somebody noticing something since there's two of them."

"What else can we do?" Chef Claire said, drying her eyes.

"I'm just waiting on an update from Sammy," Chief Abrams said.

"Sammy?" I said, frowning.

"The kid is really good with technology. Certainly a lot better than I am," Chief Abrams said. "So I asked him to do some digging into that new GPS product the dogs are wearing."

"That's a really good idea, Chief," I said. "I wish I'd thought of it."

"I'm sure you would have eventually, Suzy," he said, chuckling. "Given the way you obsess about things."

"Oh, I'll be obsessing about this one," I said, nodding. "Don't you worry about that."

We heard a knock on the kitchen door followed by the sound of someone entering without waiting for an invitation to come in. My mother joined us in the living room. She hugged Chef Claire, who immediately began sobbing again.

"Hang in there, dear," my mother said. "We are going to get them back. Aren't we, Suzy?"

"Absolutely, Mom," I said, hoping that my voice didn't reveal the uncertainty I was feeling.

My phone buzzed, and I answered it immediately.

"This is Suzy. Hey, Jackson. Great. Thanks for doing that. No, no news yet." I set my phone down and looked at Chef Claire who was staring up at me with a look of hope. "Jackson said he delivered all your bread to the restaurant."

"That was sweet of him," Chef Claire said, staring at the fireplace in a dazed haze. "That's right. I need to get to the restaurant."

I grabbed her shoulder and gently pushed her back down on the couch.

"No, you're staying here for the moment," I said. "Your staff is more than capable of handling things."

"Do you think that maybe we should just cancel Thanksgiving dinner?" Josie said.

My mother flinched at the suggestion but said nothing. I knew how much she and the rest of the town council were looking forward to putting on the event for our local residents.

"No, we can't do that," Chef Claire said. "There are too many people depending on us. We can't ruin their Thanksgiving at the last minute over something like this."

"Thank you, dear," my mother said to Chef Claire. "That's very thoughtful of you."

"No problem," Chef Claire whispered as she stood up. "I need to call the restaurant. I'll be right back."

We watched her head for her bedroom then heard another knock on the kitchen door.

"Come in," I called.

Sammy entered the living room and gave us a quick wave. He sat down at the dining room table, and we all joined him.

"What did you find out?" Chief Abrams said.

"Well, first of all, the so-called *company* that sells those GPS trackers has the worst customer service I've ever seen," Sammy said, shaking his head.

"Worse than the cable company?" Josie said.

20

Sammy snorted.

"These guys make the cable company look like Nordstrom," he said. "If I hadn't decided to just hang up, I'd still be on hold. What sort of company actually closes for Thanksgiving?"

"A small one that is very new," I said. "The sales rep who asked me to test the trackers out said that the company had developed some great technology, but that they were still in their start-up phase."

"Well, from what I could tell," Sammy said, rubbing his forehead. "I'm not sure if there is even a live person handling the phones. I was on hold for over an hour and never spoke to anybody. It was just an endless loop of automated prompts. And the reported wait time when I finally gave up was still over two hours."

"So, no ideas, huh?" I said.

"Of course I have ideas," Sammy said, smiling at me. "Just because I didn't get a chance to talk to anybody doesn't mean I didn't do anything while I was on hold."

"You're a good man, Sammy," Chief Abrams said.

"Thanks, Chief. You all know how GPS systems work, right?" he said, glancing around the table.

"Sure, sure," I said.

Josie snorted. I glared at her, but then nodded and looked at Sammy.

"But just for the sake of discussion, let's say we might need a little refresher," I said.

"Good call," Sammy said. "GPS stands for Global Positioning System. And anytime you're talking about global, that means satellites are being used to pinpoint the location of things like a building, a car, person, or, in this case, our beloved Al and Dente."

"Okay, got it," I said, gesturing for him to continue.

"But the satellites need something to fix a signal on," Sammy said. "Like the tracker you attached to the dogs' collars. And once a link between the tracker and satellite is made, you have the location pinpointed."

"But if the link is there, why aren't we getting a signal?" I said.

"Because the signal that has been made between the satellite and the tracking device needs to be sent to the app on your phone," he said. "So that means the tracking process actually involves two different signals. One between the satellite and the tracker, the second between the tracker and your phone. "

"And that's where the five-mile coverage limitation comes in," I said.

"Correct," Sammy said. "It's a tech limitation of the tracking device. I'm sure this company is aware that the signal from the device to the phone app needs a lot of work, but from the customer reviews I read, the battery in the device runs down fast and needs to be recharged on a regular basis. So my guess is that when they were designing the device, they had to make some tradeoffs between the signal strength and the life of the battery."

"How long does the battery last?" I said.

"The customer reviews said the devices work for about two days before they needed recharging," Sammy said.

"The stronger the signal, the shorter the battery life," Chief Abrams said, nodding. "That makes sense."

"So, we've hit a dead end," I whispered.

"Not at all," Sammy said. "Even though you're not getting a signal from the app on your phone, the link between the device and the satellite might still be active."

"That's interesting," Chief Abrams said. "And if it is, someone from the company should be able to access it."

"Correct. I'm sure the company collects all sorts of data on all its customers," Sammy said, glancing around the table. "You know, things like how far people are traveling with their dogs, what their favorite local places are, there's all sorts of possible data points that can be tracked and analyzed."

"Why on earth would they do that?" my mother said.

"Because that's what tech companies do," Chief Abrams said. "And you think that if we can get hold of someone at the company, they might be able to give us Al and Dente's location?"

"Yeah, that was my original thought," Sammy said, nodding.

"But since you couldn't get through to a real person, we're out of luck, right?" I said.

"Do you think I was going to give up that easily?" Sammy said.

Chef Claire entered and sat down next to me. I patted her hand.

"How are you holding up?" I said.

"Not well. What are you guys talking about?"

"I was just explaining what I've been working on," Sammy said. "I'm so sorry, Chef Claire. But we're going to get them back."

"Thanks, Sammy," Chef Claire whispered, her eyes tearing up.

"So, after I couldn't get hold of anyone at the company, I decided to take a look at their website, and we might have gotten lucky."

"How so?" Chief Abrams said, listening carefully.

"It turns out their CEO is a young guy with an adventure streak. He does things like go swimming with sharks, bungee cord drops from a thousand feet, cliff diving, all sorts of crazy stuff. His latest one is base jumping."

"Is that the one where you wear the skintight outfit that makes you look like a bat?" I said.

"That's the one," Sammy said. "You jump off a mountain and then try to navigate your way down by basically flying. Or at least as close you can come to flying wearing a bat-skin suit."

"That's insane," Josie said. "How fast do these idiots travel?"

"A hundred fifty miles an hour and up," Sammy said.

"And how do you know the CEO does stuff like this?" I said.

"It's all over their website," Sammy said. "In addition to being an adventure junkie, this guy also seems to be a megalomaniac with an ego bigger than the mountains he jumps off. He posted on the website that he's going to spend Thanksgiving base jumping in the fiords of Norway."

"Who goes to Norway for Thanksgiving," Josie said, frowning.

"I did some research and discovered that there is only one five-star resort within a hundred miles of where he plans on jumping. Since he has his own company, I figured he's probably pretty used to a luxury lifestyle. So I took a shot and called the resort. Guess who's registered."

"Well done," Chief Abram said, nodding. "If you're ever interested in a career in law enforcement, just let me know."

"No, thanks," Sammy said, shaking his head. "I'll stick with dogs."

"She manages to do both," Chief Abrams said, nodding in my direction.

"Yeah, but only because of her obsessive personality," Sammy said.

"Funny," I said.

"The resort told me the CEO was out for the day so I left a message for him to call," Sammy said, then looked at Chief Abrams. "I hope you don't mind, but I used your name and number. I thought a call from a chief of police might carry a bit more weight than one from Sammy the Dog Guy."

"That's fine," Chief Abrams said. "You think he'll call back?"

"Yeah, probably," Sammy said. "I kind of overstated the facts a bit."

"Do I want to know what you told them?" Chief Abrams said.

"Probably not," Sammy said. "But if he mentions anything about a complete and total tracking device malfunction just tell him that the message must have gotten garbled."

"Good job, Sammy," I said.

"Thanks. I was hoping that the website might have his cell phone number listed somewhere. But that was too much to ask for. Besides, the cell phone coverage in the fiords is probably awful."

A lightbulb went off in my head. I stared at Sammy, then looked at Chief Abrams.

"Uh, oh," Josie said. "She's got that look. What is it?"

"Cell phone coverage," I whispered.

"What about it?" Chief Abrams said.

"What's the one thing everyone is always complaining about around here when it comes to their cell phones?"

"All the dead zones," Josie said, nodding.

"Yeah, there's a lot of places where calls always seem to drop," my mother said.

"And you think that if we drive some of the back roads and get within the five-mile coverage area, we might be able to pick up the signal?" Chef Claire said.

"It's a longshot," I said. "But until that CEO calls back, I can't think of anything else to do."

"Let's go," Chef Claire said, getting up out of her chair.

"Hang on," I said, also getting up. "Let's get a game plan together before we head out."

I headed for a closet and rummaged around before finding what I was looking for. I headed back to the dining room and unrolled a large map that almost covered the entire table. Then I tossed a handful of Sharpies on the table.

"I bought this a few years ago," I said. "It's a topological map of the area. And all the local roads and highways are marked. I was going to have it framed, but I never got around to it."

"Should I ask why you bought that, darling?"

"I had a crazy idea about setting up a wildlife preserve," I said, embarrassed.

"She saw a National Geographic special about yaks and completely freaked out," Josie said, laughing.

"They were endangered, and I thought the climate around here would be perfect for them," I said. "But it turned out that the import restrictions on yaks were pretty hard to navigate."

"Not to mention the logistics of yak transport through the mountains of Nepal," Josie deadpanned.

"Josie?" I said.

"Yes?"

"Shut up."

"Oh, darling. We really need to find you a boyfriend."

"Funny, Mom. But forget about the yaks for now. And the boyfriend," I said, focusing on the map. "Grab one of those markers and put an X next to those places where your calls always seem to drop."

We spent the next few minutes studying and marking up the map. When we finished, we had identified four clusters we all agreed were the most common problem areas.

"Hunting areas primarily," Chief Abrams said. "They're all pretty remote, but there are a lot of access roads off the highways. Can we split them up and use more than one car?"

"No," Sammy said, shaking his head. "This is the first version of the tracking product, and the devices are limited to just one cell number."

"That's going to be a lot of driving," Chief Abrams said.

"I don't mind," Chef Claire said, again getting up out of her chair. "Let's go."

Josie and I both stood and grabbed our coats. Then I turned back to the table.

"I almost forget," I said. "We ran into Alexandra Vincent this morning and invited her to dinner. She's going to be here around seven."

"The dog show judge?" my mother said.

"Yeah, she came in a couple days early. She's a nice woman. You'll like her."

"I guess I can stay for dinner," my mother said, glancing at Sammy and Chief Abrams. "Would you gentlemen care to join me?"

"Sure," Sammy said. "What are we having?"

"There's a fresh batch of ziti in the fridge," Chef Claire said.

Josie and I both flinched. Chef Claire's ziti was one of our favorites.

"I'm happy to handle the search if you two want to stay for dinner," Chef Claire said, glancing back and forth at us.

"Not gonna happen," Josie said, shaking her head. "We can eat later."

"Yeah. And there's nothing like a drive through the countryside to work up an appetite," I said. "You want to take my car?"

"No," Josie and Chef Claire said in unison.

Chapter 4

At six the next morning, exhausted and morose, we parked behind C's and headed inside the restaurant to begin preparing Thanksgiving dinner for well over a hundred people. Josie and I sat down at the chef's table in the kitchen while Chef Claire made coffee. We waited in silence until Chef Claire returned with three steaming mugs and a tray of pastries. The coffee helped, but none of us could shake the unspoken thought that Chef Claire's dogs might be long gone.

After reviewing the map, we'd decided to begin our search in the two areas southeast of Clay Bay. The first area had taken four hours to complete, and around eight in the evening we drove to the second area that started about twenty miles out of town. The second area took much longer since there were an enormous number of small unmarked roads that switchbacked on each other. We'd gotten turned around several times and often ended up back in the same place we'd been an hour earlier. The fact that there was no moon and the sky was cloudy made navigation even more difficult, but we persevered until we finished at five without any success. We headed home, grabbed quick showers, then drove to the restaurant.

Chef Claire, still dazed, finished her coffee and stood up.

"Are you ready to get started?" she said.

"Sure. What do you need us to do?" I said, polishing off the last of a cruller that hadn't done anything to improve my mood.

"I thought you guys could help with serving once we start dinner," Chef Claire said. "But for now, I thought you could start working on the stuffing."

"And that means tearing a hundred loaves of bread into small pieces, right?" Josie said.

"Sorry," Chef Claire said, managing a small smile.

"No, that's the perfect thing for me to do right now," Josie said. "I can take out my frustrations on a bunch of defenseless bread."

"Let me know when you're done," Chef Claire said. "Right now, I need to get a dozen turkeys in the oven."

"A dozen?" I said. "Aren't you making way too much food?"

"Yeah, but I thought we'd send people home with leftovers," Chef Claire said.

We watched her slowly trudge off, and I audibly sighed.

"It's not fair," I said. "She's such a good person, and now she has to deal with the loss of her dogs."

"Let's not give up yet, okay?" Josie said.

"Okay. I'll do my best," I said, grabbing my phone. "I'm going to check in with Chief Abrams to see if that CEO has called back."

I stopped when I heard the kitchen door open, and my mother strolled in wearing an old sweater and a ratty pair of sweatpants.

She had a garment bag draped over her shoulder, and she smiled and waved at us before stopping to hug Chef Claire.

"Good morning, ladies," she said. "Any luck?"

"None," Chef Claire said, not looking up from the turkey she was struggling to get into a roasting pan.

"Hi, Mom," I said, nodding at her outfit. "When did you start taking fashion tips from me?"

"Highly unlikely, darling. Since I'll be helping out in the kitchen, I thought I'd wear my cooking clothes. I'll shower and change here before we eat."

"Good thinking," I said.

"And besides, I want to make sure I look good on TV."

Josie and I frowned, then glanced at each other.

"TV?" I said.

"Yes, darling. Didn't I mention that a television crew was going to be in town for our Thanksgiving dinner and the dog show?"

"No, Mom. I think I would have remembered that," I said, still frowning. "Just one quick question. Why?"

"Because of the publicity, darling. You know that the town council and I are very interested in extending our normal tourist season. That is the primary reason for the dog show."

"Yeah, I got that, Mom. But why would you invite them to cover Thanksgiving dinner?"

"Darling, you really need to work on your marketing and promotion skills. I can't think of a better way to promote Clay Bay as a wonderful place to live and visit than with a heartwarming human interest story of a town coming together to celebrate Thanksgiving. Especially since so many of our dinner guests would otherwise be spending the holiday alone."

She gave me her best *end of discussion* look which I completely ignored.

"Whatever happened to your constant reminders that the best charity work is done anonymously?"

"Nothing happened to it at all, darling," she said, giving me a small shrug. "And I'm so glad you took my advice to heart."

"Then why are you doing it?" I said, raising an eyebrow at her.

"It's just part of the overall story, darling."

"Gee, Mom," I said. "Why don't I believe you? What's your angle?"

"Angle? What on earth are you talking about?"

"Mom," I said, my voice rising a notch.

She stared at me, then shook her head.

"Sometimes I wish I never encouraged you to be so inquisitive. Okay, if you must know, I'm doing a favor for a friend."

"This I gotta hear," I said, folding my arms across my chest.

"As you may know, I'm a close personal friend with a certain television executive."

Among my mother's former boyfriends was a man who was the CEO of a major network. Their relationship had been short and intense, but they had parted amicably and remained good friends. And I knew that whenever my mother was in New York, they made it a point to get together for lunch or dinner. Whether their current activities went any further than that was one of those rare times when my inquisitive nature disappeared.

"And how is Bob these days?" I said.

"He's good," she said, smiling. "And he said to say hi. So, darling. Hi from Bob."

"What's the favor?"

"Well, Bob has taken, let's call it, an *active interest* in the career advancement of a reporter who works for one of his network's local affiliates."

"Which affiliate?" I said, hoping to move the discussion to a speedy conclusion.

"Syracuse."

"Who's the reporter?"

"Jessica Talbot."

"Jessica Talbot? The woman who does all those hit pieces?"

"Bob prefers the term investigative journalism."

"I'm sure he does," I said.

"That woman is a total snake," Josie said, not looking up from the huge bowl of shredded bread her hands were buried in.

"You said that Bob is taking an active interest in her career," I said. "Which translates into he's sleeping with her, right?"

34

"Darling, you know I make it a point never to insert myself into other people's private lives," my mother said. "Except yours, of course."

"Yeah, I've always liked that about you, Mom. Unbelievable. So what's Bob up to?"

"Well, he is very interested in getting Jessica to New York. Closer proximity and all that. But he's getting some serious pushback from several of his executives who consider her to be a bit of a-"

"Snake," Josie said.

"Yes, well, there is that," my mother said, nodding. "And the show that Bob has her in mind for requires someone who can pull off compassion. You know, show a softer human side."

"Which is always a challenge for a reptile," Josie said.

"Josie, please," my mother whispered.

"And you and Bob thought that a feature story about a dog show combined with a human interest piece about lonely shut-ins coming together for Thanksgiving dinner would do the trick," I said.

"Yes. I think it's called a win-win," my mother said, smiling at me. "And putting aside all of Bob's prurient and somewhat distasteful motives, you have to admit that the idea is quite brilliant."

"Brilliant isn't the word I would use, Mom."

"I know that, darling. But I'm asking both of you to play nice and go along with it. And the exposure the restaurant and the rest of the town will get isn't anything to sneeze at."

"It's not the sneezing that concerns me," Josie said. "It's the throwing up I'm worried about."

"I'm sure the infamous Ms. Talbot can't be that bad," my mother said. "Besides, she knows what's at stake, so I'm sure she'll be on her best behavior."

"Okay, Mom," I said, nodding. "But if this thing blows up, the whole town is going to blame you."

"Darling, if the garbagemen are a half-hour late on their rounds the whole town blames me."

"Yeah, you've got a good point there. What on earth did you do that's forcing you to do him a favor like this?"

"I didn't do anything. Bob bailed me out of a tricky situation several years ago, and I owe him."

"And I suppose it's a long story, right?"

"Of course," she said, smiling. "All the good ones are."

Chapter 5

The entire restaurant was filled with the aroma of Thanksgiving when our guests started arriving at eleven. Looking for anything that would keep our minds off the disappearance of Al and Dente, we had forced ourselves to stay busy then ran out of things to do as well as staff members to annoy. After everyone, including Chef Claire, had shooed us out from underfoot we gave up and headed for the lounge where our head bartender, Rocco, was setting up and keeping one eye on the football pre-game show. He lowered the volume when we sat down at the bar and held up a container of orange juice.

"Mimosa?"

"No, thanks, Rocco," I said. "Maybe later."

Josie shook her head and stifled a yawn.

"You didn't find them?"

"No, but maybe we'll have better luck this afternoon," I said.

"If you need help, just let me know," he said, sipping his coffee. "You want one of these?"

"No, thanks," I said, then shifted my weight on the bar stool and leaned forward. "You used to be a criminal, right?"

"Not guilty as charged, your honor," he said, smiling.

"Funny. Let me ask you something, what motive would someone in your former line of work have to steal dogs?"

"Well, a couple of my former colleagues stole the dogs of their former wives or girlfriends just to hurt them. The ex, not the dog. But unless Chef Claire has a disgruntled ex-whatever we don't know about, that's not the case here."

"No, she would have told us by now," I said.

"Then that leaves money, doesn't it? Has anybody contacted her about paying a ransom to get them back?"

"Nope."

"Then my guess is that whoever did it has plans to sell them, or breed them," Rocco said.

"Good luck trying to breed those two," Josie said.

"So they're selling them," Rocco said. "A couple of beautiful dogs like that would probably go for what, maybe a thousand bucks each?"

"At most," I said. "It sounds like a lot of work to make a couple grand."

"I don't know about that, Suzy," he said, popping the cork on a bottle of champagne. "If they have an established pipeline to move the dogs, it sounds pretty straightforward. How long could it have taken somebody to grab the dogs and toss them into the back of a van?"

"Not long at all," I said. "But it's still not a lot of money."

"Maybe they're making it up in volume."

"Interesting idea," I said, turning to Josie. "You haven't heard any reports of other people having their dog stolen have you?"

Josie shook her head and stifled another yawn.

We all turned when he heard the door open along with the sound of a very agitated woman's voice.

"Well, I'm sorry, Jerry. I don't like spending my Thanksgiving dealing with a bunch of local yokels any more than you do, but we made a deal, and I expect you to just shut up and do your job."

Jessica Talbot came into view. She was shorter than she appeared to be on television, but the hair and makeup were identical. She was wearing a long cashmere coat over jeans and a sweater. Standing behind her was a small man carrying a large plastic case. The man called Jerry was young and judging by the hoodie and ratty jeans, he hadn't felt the need to dress up for the occasion. Jessica squinted as her eyes adjusted to the light then saw us sitting at the bar. She strode toward us with a purpose.

"Hi, I'm Jessica Talbot," she gushed as she extended her hand.

Josie and I stared at the hand, then glanced at each other. Eventually, I gave her hand a small shake.

"Nice to meet you," I said.

"And you are?" Jessica said, giving me a smile I immediately wanted to wipe off her face.

"I'm local yokel, number thirty-one," I said. "And to my left is local yokel forty-two. That's eighty-seven behind the bar."

"Yes, I see," Jessica said, her fake smile starting to fade. "Please try not to take it personally. It's just that Jerry and I didn't expect to be here today."

"The things one has to do to advance their career, huh?"

"I beg your pardon," she said, the smile vanishing. "By the way, who are you?"

"I'm Suzy. And this is Josie. And that's Rocco."

"Yes, nice to meet all of you," she said. "I need to speak with the owner."

"Well, you're talking to two of them at the moment. The other owner is in the kitchen. But I wouldn't go in there. She's been known to throw knives at people who interrupt her when she's cooking."

"Then I guess you'll have to do," she said, glancing around the restaurant. "Jerry, go take a look around the main dining room. It looks like that might be the best spot to get what we need."

Jerry the Cameraman put the case down and wandered off. Jessica turned back to us.

"Okay, I'm thinking that we'll get some footage of people eating and chatting during dinner. I'm looking for something that says...*homey*."

"Good word," Josie said.

"Yeah, but I think homey might be a bit of a stretch for her to pull off," I said.

"Yup. But still easier than her trying to come across as human," Josie said, staring at Jessica.

40

"Do we have a problem here?" Jessica said, glancing back and forth at us.

"Not yet," I said. "But the day's young."

"I'm sorry, but I don't understand the hostility. One would think that someone with my reputation showing up to do a feature piece on your restaurant might be met with at least a modicum of gratitude."

"Modicum. Another good word," Josie said.

"Not bad. But I've always preferred smidgen," I said.

"Okay, so that's the way it's going to be all day, huh?" Jessica said.

"Oh, please tell me you're not planning on being here all day," Josie deadpanned.

"I don't think I like you," Jessica said, flipping her hair back with a head nod.

"Well, now we officially have something in common, don't we?" Josie said.

"What is it? Some sort of personal jealousy about my success? Or maybe you don't like some of the stories I've done."

"We don't like any of the stories you've done," I said.

"Well, I guess that's why they call it a free country," Jessica said, rediscovering her fake smile. "Everyone is entitled to their opinion. But all the awards hanging on my office wall tell a different story. I've got a dozen."

"Yeah, but how many did you have to buy yourself?" Josie deadpanned.

41

"Oh, good one," I said, laughing.

"Tell me, Jessica," Josie said. "Did you win an award for the hit piece you did on welfare reform?"

"It wasn't a hit piece. But, no, I didn't," she whispered.

"Was that because your former cameraman told your boss you planted the three grand that just happened to be on the floor while you were interviewing that woman in the conference room, right?" I said.

"That's an unfounded rumor," Jessica snapped.

"And when she slid the envelope into her purse after you stepped out for a minute, you got it all on tape."

"That woman was a thief."

"No, Jessica," Josie said. "She was a destitute single mom trying to feed five kids. She made a mistake, but you felt compelled to show it on TV."

"That doesn't excuse the behavior. The fraud in our welfare system totals in the billions. It's not my fault that people make stupid choices all the time."

"Speaking of people who make stupid choices, how is Bob?" I said, smiling at her.

She flinched but recovered quickly.

"Bob? Bob who?"

"Nice try. Tell me, is Bob still conducting his job interviews horizontally?"

"You don't want to mess with me," Jessica said, her nostrils flaring.

"You're right, Jessica. I don't," I said. "So, if you and your cameraman want to head out, that would be just fine. I'm sure you and Bob can come up with another way to try to humanize you."

"Nothing would please me more," she said, again doing the head flip to get the hair out of her eyes. "But I have a job to do. And that includes doing at least one interview with a local yo-…representative. Please tell me it won't be you."

"No, that would be my mother."

"And your mother is?"

"Going to pay dearly for this," I said.

"You're really not funny," Jessica said.

"Disagree. That was a good one," Josie said.

"Thanks," I said to Josie before refocusing on Jessica. "My mother is the mayor of Clay Bay."

"How lovely for her," she said. "Let me guess. In her spare time, she likes to whittle on the front porch."

"Just a friendly piece of advice, Jessica. You do not want to cross swords with my mother."

"I'll keep that in mind," she said, returning my stare.

"Okay, but don't say I didn't warn you."

"Where is she?" Jessica said, glancing around.

"She hasn't arrived yet. But don't worry, you'll know when she does."

"Then if you'll excuse me, I have some prep work to do," Jessica said, shifting her bag to the other shoulder. "I'd like to say it's been a pleasure meeting you, but I think we know it hasn't.

Lucky for all of us, this will be the last time we'll be running into each other."

"Actually, that's not the case, Jessica," I said.

"Really? Why on earth not?"

"Because you'll be seeing us at the dog show," Josie said.

"Oh, you're dog people. I should have known."

"So, on top of everything else, you don't like dogs," I said.

"I hate dogs," she said. "They're the epitome of cloying loyalty and misguided obedience. I get more than enough of that from the men in my life. I much prefer the unwavering indifference I get from my cat."

"Smart cat," Josie said.

"Clever. So, you bought tickets to the big dog show. That's sweet. You two are quite the social climbers, huh?"

"Actually, no," Josie said. "We're the main sponsor."

"I see. Just my luck. My producer goes to Hawaii, and I get stuck with the Yokel Twins."

She shook her head and walked away.

"So, she hates dogs, huh?" Josie said, smiling.

"Yeah," I said, nodding. "That could come in handy."

"You know, one of you is probably going to have to agree to do an interview with her at the dog show," Rocco said.

"Now you talk?" I said, turning to him.

"I was having too much fun listening," he said, laughing. "Remind me never to argue with you two."

"He's right," Josie said. "One of us will probably need to be on camera with her."

"You do it."

"No way. It's your turn," Josie said, shaking her head.

"How is it my turn? We've never done a television interview before."

"I'm referring to doing things we both hate."

"And?"

"And I did the last one."

"Which was?"

"It'll come to me in a minute," Josie said.

"You're the vet."

"So?"

"It's an interview about dogs. So, you should do it."

"I'll arm wrestle you for it."

"No way. Last time you almost broke my wrist."

"Rock, paper, scissors?"

"No, I can never keep it straight what does what to what."

"What does what to what? Are you faking a sudden onset of Tourettes?"

"Funny. Rocco will flip a coin."

"Why Rocco?"

"Because you cheat," I said.

"Just that one time," Josie said.

Rocco, still laughing, grabbed a quarter from his tip jar.

"Call it in the air," he said, flipping the coin.

"Heads," Josie said.

We both watched as Rocco removed his hand to reveal tails.

"Hah," Josie chortled.

"I don't want to talk to that woman."

"Tell you what. All you need to do is modify that old public speaking trick during the interview," Josie said, laughing.

"I'm going to need a little clarification."

"Instead of picturing the audience as being naked to help you relax, just imagine Jessica bleeding profusely from several well-placed wounds, and you'll be fine."

"That doesn't help."

"Disagree. Just imagine the possibilities."

Chapter 6

By the time we joined my mother at her table, the restaurant was full, the food was hot, and I was still steaming. I sat down between my mother and Alexandra and waited until members of our local clergy led us in prayer. Then I filled my plate and focused on my food. Josie quickly found her form and Alexandra watched with a look I can only describe as bewildered amazement as Josie demonstrated her capabilities with a knife and fork. Eventually, Josie sensed eyes on her, and she looked across the table at Alexandra.

"Yes?" Josie said, casually.

"I was just admiring the way you handle your utensils," she said, embarrassed.

"Well, I'm a vet. So, I know how to handle a knife."

"Yes, I can see that," Alexandra said. "That's a prodigious amount of food you've got there."

"Prodigious. Good word," Josie said, refocusing on her plate.

Alexandra continued to stare across the table in disbelief.

"What can I say?" Josie said, pausing to glance up at Alexandra. "Dealing with pond scum always makes me hungry."

"Josie, please," my mother said. "That's enough."

"You invited her, Mrs. C.," Josie said, shrugging at my mother. "That makes her your problem."

"She's someone all of us need to deal with," my mother said, then caught herself. "Not that she's a problem, of course."

Josie snorted and spooned another helping of stuffing onto her plate, then passed the bowl to Jackson who was sitting next to her.

"Help me out here, darling," my mother said. "Jessica isn't that bad, right?"

"Mom, I'd rather be forced to watch football all day," I said. "And that's enough chatter about the Death Adder. It's putting me off my food."

"You're a big help," my mother said.

"Drop it, Mom. You're in enough trouble with me already."

"It's just because of the missing dogs," my mother said to Alexandra. "Normally, my daughter is one of the sweetest people you'll ever meet."

"It's quite all right," Alexandra said. "I'm familiar with that woman's work. Pond scum may actually be too kind of a description."

"There you go," I said, brandishing my fork. "Thank you, Alexandra."

"You're welcome, dear," she said. "Did you help cook this delicious meal?"

"We just helped with the stuffing," I said.

"Bread ripping duty," Josie said.

"I see," Alexandra said, puzzled. "Well, good job. The sage is easy to pick up, but I'm getting a hint of something else."

"I think it's nutmeg," I said. "It's one of Chef Claire's favorites."

"Did I hear you say that you are resuming your search for the dogs this afternoon?" Alexandra said.

"Right after dinner," I said, glaring at Jerry the Cameraman who was hovering and filming near our table.

"Despicable people," Alexandra said. "I'm not sure what I would do if someone stole my dogs."

"I'd like to grab a kitchen knife and bury it in their chest," I said. "People like that don't deserve to be walking around wasting all the oxygen."

Alexandra chuckled and resumed eating.

"Are you going to need any help today, darling?"

"No thanks, Mom. You've done more than enough for one day."

"My, my. This is quite the hissy fit. You need to let it go, Suzy."

It was one of her best voices: One part compassion; two parts warning. And whenever she called me by my name, I knew she was close to boiling over. I thought about it for a moment, then chose to ignore her.

"Let it go? Mom, I haven't even started."

"We'll discuss this later, young lady."

I flinched but quickly recovered. Still, I knew she caught it. I returned her crocodile smile and nodded at her.

"You can bet on that, Mom."

Jessica wandered across the room toward our table. I wiped my face with a napkin, took a sip of water, then stood.

"Please, excuse me. I'm going to mingle."

"Don't let me run you off," Jessica said, laughing.

"That's okay," I said, nodding at Jerry the Cameraman. "I wouldn't want to be caught on camera doing anything untoward."

"Good word," Jessica said to my back.

I headed straight for Chief Abrams table. I said hello to his family, then gestured that I'd like a quiet word. He followed me into the lounge.

"Any word from the CEO yet?" I said.

"No," Chief Abrams said. "I hope he didn't crash into the side of a mountain."

"Now there's an idea," I said. "Maybe I could convince her to give base jumping a shot."

"What?"

"Nothing. I'm just babbling."

"It's the reporter, right?"

"Yeah. I started the day with a strong dislike for her, but after I met her, it quickly morphed into an intense hatred."

"She's something else," he said, shaking his head. "She must have been briefed about the rash of recent murders in town because the first words out of her mouth were to ask me if anybody had died today."

"And?" I said, raising an eyebrow.

"I patted my gun, gave her my best cop look, and said not yet, but the day's young."

"Good for you," I said, laughing. "My mother is so gonna pay for this."

"Try to go easy on her," Chief Abrams said, giving me a fatherly look I recognized and still missed. "She's just trying to get the town some much needed positive PR. A lot of the business folks and the town council are getting nervous that all the murders might start impacting tourist season."

"As long as nobody figures out a way to drain the River, I don't think we need to worry about that."

"Yeah, probably. But you know what happens when people start worrying."

"Are you?"

"Me? Worried? That's not gonna happen. If they try messing with me, I'll just start my new career as a beer drinking fisherman. Until then, as long as they keep making criminals, I'll be doing my best to catch them. Speaking of which, are you still planning to resume your search this afternoon?"

"Just as soon as we can get out of here."

"Well, if you need anything, just give me a call."

"Will do. Thanks, Chief."

"Are you ever going to be comfortable calling me by my first name?" he said, laughing.

"I doubt it."

"That's what I thought. Okay, it looks like dessert is being served. Any suggestions?"

"Well, I always like to go for a lot of all of it."

"Good call. Later."

I watched him walk away, then glanced at the bar. It took me a minute to recognize the man with his back to me who was chatting with Rocco, then I smiled and approached.

"Rooster," I said, placing a hand on his massive shoulder. "I didn't know you were here. Thanks for coming."

Rooster Jennings swiveled around on his barstool and returned my hug. Rooster was a local resident and longtime friend who liked to be left alone and usually avoided social gatherings like they were communicable diseases. Most other people were more than happy to return the favor. But since we'd opened the restaurant, he'd become somewhat of a regular. Despite the fact that we were lifelong friends, I'd decided that Rooster's recent willingness to socialize had more to do with Chef Claire's cooking than it did with our relationship. He ran a year-round small engine repair business on the water and expanded his operation during the summer to include the sale of gas and sundries to tourists at outrageous prices. A devout dog person, Rooster had adopted one of the German Shepherd puppies we rescued from an illegal puppy mill operating in the area several months ago.

I ran my hand along the lapel of the suit he was wearing and shook my head. Normally, Rooster's fashion choice didn't extend past grimy jeans and tee shirts and a pair of old boots he wore without laces or socks.

"Did you dress up just for me, Rooster?"

"You caught me," he said, beaming at me. "The things I do for you, right?"

"Well, I'm glad you came."

"This is a wonderful thing you're doing today," Rooster said, staring at me. "A lot of people are going to remember this Thanksgiving for a long time."

"Thanks," I said. "Unfortunately, it's going to be memorable for another reason."

"Yes, I'm sure," he said, his expression turning dark. "Rocco and I were just talking about what we'd like to do to the people who stole Chef Claire's dogs. Any luck yet?"

"No, but we're heading out soon to give it another shot."

"You call me if you need anything, Suzy."

"I will, Rooster. Thanks. Say, how's Titan doing?"

"He's magnificent," Rooster said, beaming. "Smart, loyal, strong as an ox, and able to scare the crap out of mouthy tourists whenever I tell him to."

Rocco and I both laughed.

"You should have entered him in the dog show," I said. "Maybe they have *best at dealing with mouthy tourists* as one of their prizes."

"I don't need validation from anybody else about what a great dog I have."

He stated it as a simple truth. I smiled and nodded at him. "Spoken like a true dog person," I said.

Chapter 7

I headed back to the table to collect Josie and say goodbye to my mother. On the way, I saw Alexandra at another table chatting with several people I didn't know. She waved me over, and I stood next to the table and glanced around.

"Suzy, I'd like you to meet some folks who are in town for the dog show," Alexandra said. "Like me, they didn't have formal plans for Thanksgiving, so they decided to come in a few days early."

"It's nice to meet you," I said, smiling but anxious to get on the road.

"This is Glenn and Abby Wilson. They'll be showing their wonderful Chesapeake Bay retriever. He's already won five Best in Group awards."

"Six," the man said, smiling at Alexandra.

"And don't forget the Best in Show Monty won last month," Abby said.

"Of course," Alexandra said, her eyes narrowing just a touch. "Silly me."

"Since you're judging the show, Alexandra," Abby said. "I'm assuming you won't be entering either of your Goldens."

"No, I'll just be judging the competition," Alexandra said.

I couldn't miss the tension between the two women and looked back and forth at them.

"That's what I hoped you'd say," Abby said. "I must say that I'm pleasantly surprised with your sense of fair play."

"Yes, that's what I thought," Alexandra said, breaking into a wide smile. "And since I'm not showing any of my dogs, that might just provide you with an opportunity to win, Abby."

Nice shot, Alexandra. Right across the bow and it caught Abby and Glenn right between the eyes. They both twitched in their chairs. Glenn was the first to recover.

"Yes, well," he said. "You're track record speaks for itself, Alexandra. I guess we should all thank you for your generosity in not entering the competition."

Alexandra's eyes twinkled, and she moved on to continue with the introductions. A few minutes later, while I could easily recall the names and breeds of each dog mentioned, I forgot all the people's names almost immediately. Alexandra worked her way around the table until we landed on an elegant woman in her sixties who was smiling up at me with the brightest blue eyes I'd seen in a long time.

"Sitting next to Glenn is Margaret Jackson. Margaret breeds and shows the most delightful Springer Spaniels I've ever seen."

"Oh, I love Springers," I said.

"Then you're going to love Maggie," she said, beaming. "This is a wonderful restaurant. I understand that it's open year round."

"It is."

"And you're one of the owners."

Even though she seemed like a very nice person, my snoop-alert alarm went off.

"Yes," I said. "But all the credit goes to the majority owner, Chef Claire. She designed it, and does pretty much all the work."

"So, your participation is somewhat limited," Margaret said.

"Yes. Limited to eating and writing checks, primarily," I said, laughing.

"Well, I think it's a wonderful addition," she said. "This town can certainly use another year-round establishment."

Her second reference to year-round caught my attention.

"I take it you've been to Clay Bay before," I said.

"Actually, I used to live here," she said, smiling. "A long time ago."

"Really?"

"Yes, but I left after my divorce," she said, taking a sip of her Mimosa.

"I see."

I ran her last name through my memory bank but came up empty.

"I'm sorry, but I don't remember the Jackson family," I said, frowning.

"Jackson was my maiden name," she said, smiling. "Which I was more than delighted to reacquire after my divorce. My married name was Jennings."

I stared at her and wondered if my mouth had dropped open. I recovered and cocked my head at her.

"Rooster? You were married to Rooster Jennings?"

"Yes," she said, nodding. "I can see you're familiar with him." Margaret glanced around to include everyone else at the table in the conversation. "My ex-husband was quite the local character. I think the term most people used was hermit. He was a good man with many wonderful qualities. It's just too bad that Rooster felt compelled to keep everyone, myself included, at a distance and his true self buried under several layers of dirt and grease."

Her use of the past tense was impossible to miss, but I stayed silent and waited for her to continue.

"I got news that he passed several years ago, and I've never been able to get past the memories, so I stayed away. When I heard about the dog show the town had organized, I finally decided enough time had passed and that it was silly for me not to enjoy this beautiful part of the country. So, here I am."

"Here you are," I said, managing a weak smile. "Well, I'd like to welcome all of you, and I'm looking forward to seeing you and your dogs at the show."

I caught Josie's eye and gestured that I'd be there in a minute, then waved goodbye to the table and headed straight for the lounge. Rooster and Rocco were in the middle of a shared laugh. Rooster caught my approach out of the corner of his eye and swiveled toward me.

"You're back already?" he said.

"Yeah, I just met someone in the restaurant."

"Are you okay?" Rocco said. "You look like you've seen a ghost."

"Closer than you might think," I said.

"What?" Rocco said, frowning at me.

"I'm just babbling," I said, then smiled at Rooster. "All these years, you've been holding out on me."

"Oh, no," Rooster said. "You've got that look."

"What look is that?"

"The look that says there's a mystery lurking that needs to be solved," he said, laughing.

"Lurking. Good word," I said, smiling at him. "I'm not sure I'd call this one a mystery. But I've got a whole bunch of questions I'd love to have answered."

"Go ahead, Suzy. You know our deal," he said, giving me his undivided attention. "You can ask me anything you want, but I get to choose which ones I'm gonna answer."

"I know the rules, Rooster. I guess my first question is why didn't you ever tell me you used to be married?"

Rooster flinched but remained calm. Eventually, he shrugged.

"I guess it's just because it never came up. It was a long time ago, it didn't last long, and I heard she died several years ago. And I'm the sort of person who doesn't much like to dwell on the past."

Now I was thoroughly confused. For two people that were supposed to be dead, they certainly appeared to be in pretty good shape to me.

"Can I ask why you're asking me that question now?" Rooster said.

"Sure," I said, frowning as my brain began to redline. "It was something that somebody mentioned a few minutes ago."

"By the stranger you just met in the dining room?"

"Yes."

"And this person gave you the impression they know me?"

"Most definitely."

"And you were surprised by the conversation," Rooster said.

"Very much so."

"Will I be?"

"Surprised?" I said, raising an eyebrow at him. "Surprised is definitely a word for it, Rooster."

"Okay. So who is this mysterious stranger supposed to be?"

"Your ex-wife."

Chapter 8

Two hours later, we came to a stop when we reached the same spot we'd been at twenty minutes earlier. The compacted dirt trails intersected, then branched out again like spider veins. I glanced down at the map again, then sighed.

"This thing is useless," I said. "None of these dirt roads are mapped. That's the problem."

"I'd tell you to check your phone for the location," Josie deadpanned. "But there's no cell coverage out here."

"Yes, I know," I snapped. "Hence, the problem."

"Don't yell at me," Josie snapped back.

"Who else am I going to yell at?"

"Yeah, you got a point there," she said, laughing. "Geez, what a mess."

"I thought you grew up around here," Chef Claire said, drumming her fingers on the steering wheel.

"I grew up on the River," I said. "In case you haven't noticed, I don't spend a lot of time in the woods."

"Yes, I've noticed," Chef Claire said. "The last two days have made that abundantly clear."

"Don't you start."

"Enough, please," Josie said. "We just need to think this through. We've almost covered this entire section, so let's try to focus and get this done. I think we need to turn left here."

"No, I was thinking we need to make a right," Chef Claire said, shaking her head.

"You want to cast the deciding vote?" Josie said to me.

"Actually, what I want to do is find Al and Dente and get the heck out of here."

"Well, we're not going to find them sitting here," Josie said, fidgeting in the back seat. "I can't believe Rooster used to be married."

"I can't believe they both thought the other one was dead," I said.

"I wonder who told them that," Chef Claire said.

"My guess is it was someone who wanted to eliminate the possibility that they could ever get back together," I said.

"Ooooooh," Josie said. "Possibly unrequited love from afar. Always a good one."

"Or maybe someone carrying a grudge," I said. "But it's odd and-"

"Wait a sec. Is that right?" Josie said.

I turned around and saw the frown on her face.

"Is what right?"

"Carrying a grudge? I thought it was holding a grudge," Josie said.

"Carry. Hold. What's the difference?" I snapped.

"Carrying implies movement," she said.

"Unbelievable," I said, shaking my head.

"Speaking of movement," Chef Claire said. "I'm turning right."

She did, and we started up a small incline. My phone buzzed.

"How about that?" I said, answering the call. "Cell phone reception. Hey, Chief. What's up? Ah, the call dropped."

I looked through the windshield and noticed that we were definitely going up an incline.

"Keep going," I said. "Maybe we'll be able to get some reception at the top of this hill."

We slowly made our way up the rough road until we reached a clearing at the top. I called the number and waited for Chief Abrams to answer.

"Where are you guys?" he said.

"I think we're on the road to nowhere," I said.

"Good song," he said. "Talking Heads, right?"

"Did you call to discuss karaoke options, or is there a point to this conversation?" I said.

"Your mom was right. It's a full on hissy fit," he said.

"Sorry. It's been a long day," I said. "And it's not a hissy fit."

Josie snorted in the backseat.

"Let's go, people," Chef Claire said, still drumming the steering wheel.

"The CEO finally called me back," Chief Abrams said.

"That's great," I said. "What did he have to say?"

"I haven't spoken to him yet. But I've got him on hold on the other line. Since you're already out there, if he does have any news, I thought we might be able to save some time by trying a three-way call. Put your phone on speaker."

"That's a great idea, Chief."

"Yeah, I have my moments," he said. "Hang on. Just give us a minute."

"Us?" I said.

"Sammy's here. You don't think I was going to try to get this call set up on my own, do you?"

We sat quietly, then he came back on the line.

"Okay, I think we got it," Chief Abrams said. "Mr. Claudine, are you there?"

"I'm here."

The call was so clear Mr. Claudine could have been in the backseat. But he sounded very groggy.

"I have three people on the other line. I'd like to introduce Suzy, Josie and Chef Claire."

"Hello, ladies. It's nice to meet you. I'm sorry to hear about your dogs."

"Thank you," Chef Claire said.

"Are you okay, Mr. Claudine?" Chief Abrams said. "You sound kind of out of it."

"It's the painkillers the hospital has me on," he said, laughing. "They're quite good if you know what I mean."

"I do," Chief Abrams said. "You're in the hospital?"

"Yes. I had a minor base jumping accident."

"With all due respect, sir," Chief Abrams said. "I've seen base jumping videos. How is it possible for any accident associated with that activity to be considered minor?"

"Compared to some of the other possibilities, Chief Abrams, trust me, my mishap was definitely minor," he said, coughing then clearing his throat. "I was about to finish a wonderful jump off one of the fiords when I got a bit cocky and decided I would try, in the parlance of gymnastics, to stick the landing."

"And I take it you didn't stick it?" Chief Abrams said.

"Actually, I completed what I consider a partial stick," he said, giggling.

Either this guy had the sunniest disposition on the planet, or the drugs he was on were out of this world.

"I'm not following, sir," Chief Abrams said.

"My feet stuck, but, unfortunately, the rest of my body didn't. I snapped both ankles on impact. My doctor likened it to eating a roast chicken. You know, like when you remove one of the legs."

All three of us in the car grimaced.

"Yeah, I got it," Chief Abrams said. "That must hurt like hell."

"I'm sure it will at some point," Mr. Claudine said, still laughing. "Now, before I completely drift off, I have some information for you. Do you have something to write with?"

"I do. Whenever you're ready."

"Okay, one of my lead technicians took a look at the coordinates of the two tracking devices. Unfortunately, both of the batteries have completely discharged."

"Oh, no," Chef Claire whispered.

I handed her a tissue to wipe her eyes as I focused on the call.

"Hang in there," I whispered.

"But he was able to recover the coordinates from the last transmission between one of the devices and our satellite. Why we weren't able to recover any coordinates from the second device, I'm not sure. My guess is that it was either disabled or perhaps it was submerged in water. We're still doing everything we can to improve the waterproofing, but we still have a long way to go."

We heard a long, deep yawn on the other end of the line.

"Maybe you should give me those coordinates, Mr. Claudine," Chief Abrams said. "You sound pretty sleepy."

"I think the word you're looking for is zonked, Chief Abrams," he said, giggling. "I'm totally zonked. Zonked. That's a good word, wouldn't you say?"

"Yeah. Good word," Chief Abrams said, his patience starting to wear a bit thin. "The coordinates, please, sir."

"Yes, of course, the coordinates. Now, where did I put them? Oh, there they are. Right in my hand the whole time."

We listened as he read a series of numbers. I didn't bother writing them down since there was no way we'd be able to make any sense of them or translate them into a specific location.

"All you'll need to do is input those coordinates into any of the apps that convert GPS into an actual location," Mr. Claudine said.

"That's all I need to do, huh?" Chief Abrams said.

I smiled as I pictured Chief Abrams scratching his head.

"I know how to do that," Sammy interjected. "Piece of cake. And that's not a suggestion, Josie."

"Funny," Josie said.

"Thanks for your help, Mr. Claudine," Chief Abrams said. "We really appreciate it."

"No problem. Good luck finding the dogs. And if you need anything else, just let me know. You'll know where to find me for the next few weeks. And I don't think you'll need to use a tracking device."

For some reason, he found his last comment especially funny, and his portion of the call finished with him still cackling on the other end of the line.

"Give us a minute," Chief Abrams said. "Sammy's on it."

"I hope it's nearby," Chef Claire said, now gripping the steering wheel with both hands.

"Well, what do you know?" Chief Abrams said.

"What?" I said.

"Do you remember when we were dealing with all the craziness Rooster's brother and cousin got us into last year?"

Last winter, a Dandie Dinmont we'd found had been stolen from the Inn, and we'd eventually tracked it down at a hunting camp Rooster owned about twenty miles outside of Clay Bay. Chief Abrams description of the events was accurate. The whole situation had been crazy.

"Of course," I said.

"Well, these coordinates point to a spot about two miles from that hunting camp," Chief Abrams said.

Chef Claire started the engine, turned around, and we began bouncing our way down the rough road. Josie and I both held on for dear life as Chef Claire made her way back toward the highway.

"It looks like it's about a quarter mile up and to the left of the access road," Chief Abrams said. "Did Rooster say anything about his brother being back in town when you were talking to him at the restaurant?"

"No, but I can't blame him for not mentioning it. I'm pretty sure he had something else on his mind," I said.

"Good story?"

"Without a doubt," I said.

"Any details worth sharing at the moment?" he said.

"Not yet. But stay tuned. Rooster knows those woods like the back of his hand so you might want to give him a call."

"Just as soon as we finish this one," he said. "I'll get out there as soon as I can. And if you see anything that looks suspicious or even remotely dangerous, promise you'll wait for me."

I glanced at Chef Claire who shook her head no and gripped the steering wheel even tighter.

"Suzy?"

"Yes."

"Do you promise?"

"Yes. I promise."

"Suzy?"

"Yes, Chief?"

"You've got your fingers crossed, don't you?"

"Yeah."

Chapter 9

The drive to the access road that led to Rooster's camp took about twenty minutes. Just before we made the turn off the highway, I glanced through the passenger side rear view mirror and noticed a black SUV with tinted windows about a hundred yards behind us. I glanced over at Chef Claire who was also keeping an eye on the SUV.

"How long have they been following us?" I said.

"I noticed the car just after we got back on the highway," Chef Claire said. "It looks like something somebody from the government would drive."

"Yeah, it does," I said. "Why on earth would they be following us?"

"No idea," she said. "And at the moment, I really don't care. I just want to find my dogs."

We turned off the highway and bounced our way up the dirt access road until Chef Claire slammed on the brakes and turned the car off. We hopped out and glanced around the dense woods. The wind was starting to pick up, and the temperature was dropping. There was only about a half-hour of daylight left, so I grabbed flashlights and our binoculars from my bag, and we began a slow walk toward the spot Chief Abrams had pointed us to.

"Al! Dente!" Chef Claire called several times.

The only responses she got back were faint echoes. I glanced back at the highway and didn't see any sign of the black SUV.

"I guess they weren't following us," I said, resuming my search as we moved through the brown, withered brush.

Chef Claire continued to call the dogs' names as we slowly made our way forward. We began walking in a wide circle that became smaller with each pass we made and carefully examined the ground. Ten minutes later, Chef Claire stopped and started crying.

"They're not here," she said. "But at least we didn't find their bodies."

"Don't talk like that," I whispered. "I'm sure they're okay."

"But they're not here," Chef Claire said, her shoulders shaking as she continued to sob.

"No, but they were," Josie said, staring down at the ground. "At least Al was."

"What are you talking about?" Chef Claire said.

"That," Josie said, pointing.

Sticking out of the large pile were the remnants of a red dog collar and one of the tracking devices. Chef Claire knelt down and used a stick to extract the collar and device from the relatively fresh clue Al had left behind.

"It's Al's collar," Chef Claire said. "Or at least what's left of it."

"How the heck did he get it off?" I said.

"I don't know how he does it," she said, smiling. "That's the third one this month he's managed to destroy."

"He's quite the chewer," I said.

"Yes, and quite prolific in other areas," Josie said, staring down at the large pile. "Now what?"

"Hunting camp," I said. "It's the perfect spot to hide out."

"Let's go," Chef Claire said.

I did my best to keep up with her and Josie, but by the time the outline of the camp was visible through the trees, I was a hundred feet behind and completely winded. Josie and Chef Claire ducked down behind a thicket. Eventually, I caught up with them and dropped to my knees gasping for air.

"What do you think?" Chef Claire said.

"I think I need to get to the gym," I said, rolling over onto my back.

Josie snorted but kept staring at the hunting camp through her binoculars.

"There's definitely somebody there. The lights are on, and there's smoke coming out of the chimney."

"How do you want to do this?" Chef Claire said. "We can't just knock on the door."

"Maybe we should split up and do some reconnaissance before we try to do anything," I said, pushing myself back up into a kneeling position. "If I remember, there are two doors in the back. Josie and I will check them out while you keep an eye on the front. We don't have much time before it gets dark, so let's meet back at this spot in fifteen minutes."

"Okay," Chef Claire said. "Do we need some sort of signal?"

"Good idea," I said, nodding. "How about we whistle? One whistle means to head back to the spot. Two means we're going inside the camp."

"Got it," Chef Claire said.

"Be careful," I said.

"And try not to kill anybody," Josie said to Chef Claire.

"I'm not making any promises," she said.

Josie and I worked our way through the trees until the back of the camp was about fifty feet in front of us. We heard movement and the muffled sound of voices coming from inside.

"Can you make anything out?" Josie whispered.

"No, we're going to have to get a bit closer."

"Let's make our way over to that storage shed," I said, pointing, then froze in my tracks. "Wait. I see someone."

"Where?"

"Behind that tree over there on the left," I whispered.

"Yeah, I see him. It looks like he's also trying to figure out what's going on inside," Josie said. "What the heck is he doing here?"

I thought about it, then a lightbulb went off.

"The black SUV," I said. "I guess they were following us after all."

"He's a big dude. What do you want to do?"

"Well, there are two of us," I said.

"Yes, but given the size of him," Josie said. "That would make the odds what, two against four?"

"What do you suggest?"

"I suppose running is out of the question."

"Let's call that plan B," I whispered. "Hang on. I think I have them with me." I rummaged through my backpack and help up a pair of handcuffs.

"Handcuffs? Is there something about your personal life you've been keeping from me, Suzy?"

"Funny. Chief Abrams gave them to me."

"For what?"

"For times like this," I whispered. "Grab that piece of firewood over there, and we'll sneak up behind him. You bop him on the head, and when he goes down, I'll cuff him."

"Just like that?"

"Just like that," I said, nodding.

"I think we should go with plan B."

"We need to find Al and Dente," I said. "Come on. Let's get this over with."

I was pretty sure she was glaring at me, but I couldn't be sure in the fading light. She picked up a chunk of wood about the size of a softball bat and followed me as I tiptoed my way toward the large man whose back was to us. As we got closer, he seemed laser-focused on what was going on inside the camp.

When I was five feet behind him, I could hear him breathing.

I took another step closer and felt Josie right behind my left shoulder. I slowly took a step to the right to get out of the way of Josie's swing and stepped on a twig. All three of us heard it snap and the man flinched, then began to turn around.

"Now!" I shouted and gripped the handcuffs with both hands.

Josie launched into her swing, then recognized the face and tried to pull back. But her momentum carried her forward, and the chunk of firewood bounced off Rooster's forehead. He dropped to one knee, then stared at us with a dazed look.

"Rooster," Josie whispered. "I'm so sorry."

"Geez, that hurts," he said, rubbing the spot. "What the hell is wrong with you two?"

"Actually, there are a lot of theories floating around about that," I said. "Rooster, I'm sorry. We had no idea that was you."

The back door of the camp opened, and a man's head poked through. In the darkness, it was impossible to see his face.

"What is it? Is somebody out there?" a woman called from inside.

"No," the man said. "It's probably just that raccoon."

The door closed, and we refocused on Rooster. He was wiping blood off his forehead and still glaring at Josie.

"What are you doing out here?" I said.

"I'm looking for my idiot brother. What's your excuse?"

"We're looking for Chef Claire's dogs," Josie said.

"And you think they're here?" Rooster said.

"It's a definite possibility," I said. "I didn't know your brother was back in town."

"That makes two of us," he said.

"What do you think he's up to?" I said.

"He's undoubtedly trying to make time with my ex-wife."

Another lightbulb went off.

"He's the one who told you and Margaret that the other one was dead?"

"That's what she told me at the restaurant," he said, stuffing the bloody handkerchief into his pocket.

"Quite the surprise reunion, huh?" I said. "Why would your brother do something like that?"

"He always had the hots for her. Now I find out that he's stayed in touch with her all these years."

"Have they been, you know, having a relationship?" I said.

"That's what I'm here to find out," Rooster said, standing up. "Margaret says no, but I'm not sure if I can believe a word coming out of her mouth."

"Did you recognize either of those voices?" I said.

"No, I didn't."

"Well, if Chef Claire's dogs are in there, they must be working with your brother, right?"

"Yeah, probably," he said, then glared at Josie. "You could have killed me."

"I'm sorry, Rooster. I tried to stop my swing, but-"

"Yeah, I got it."

"After the way you threatened your brother the last time when they stole the dog from the Inn I was sure they'd never do it again," I said.

"What can I say? My brother and cousin have always been slow learners."

"Your cousin? Coke Bottle is here?"

Coke Bottle was the nickname we'd given to Rooster's cousin because of the thick glasses he wore. Without them, he had a hard time seeing past his face.

"Yeah, I heard him earlier," he said. "I have no idea who the other two are. By the way, where's Chef Claire?"

"She's watching the front," I said. "So, what's the plan?"

"Well, now that I know the dogs might be in there, we need to be careful. Once we get in there, follow my lead. And if we see any signs of guns, I'd prefer it if you two made yourself scarce. Got it?"

We both nodded in the dark.

"I repeat, got it?"

"Sorry," I said. "We were nodding."

"There's a door on the side that leads into the back bedroom. We'll slip inside and try to get a handle on things before we do anything else. Once I get the door open, you'll see a small alcove off to the right. We'll hide there and just listen for a while."

"What if the door's locked?" Josie whispered.

Rooster jangled a set of keys.

"Oops, I forgot," she said. "Never mind."

We followed Rooster as he slowly made his way toward the camp.

"What if the door's locked," I said, with a whispered laugh.

"Shut up."

We made our way up the small set of steps and waited as Rooster silently unlocked and opened the door. Moments later, we were huddled inside a dark and cramped alcove.

"Where did you find these two idiots anyway?" the woman said.

"They were recommended by Geno," the man said.

"Who's Geno?" Coke Bottle said.

"Geno. The guy we drink with a couple nights a week at The Lay About," Rooster's brother said. "You do remember him, right?"

"That's his name?" Coke Bottle said. "I thought it was Buddy."

"What?"

"That's what everybody in the bar calls him. Every time he comes in people always say 'Hey, buddy.' 'How ya doing, buddy?'"

"She's right. You are an idiot," Rooster's brother said.

"Unbelievable," the woman said. "You've outdone yourself this time."

"Don't start on me," the man snapped. "Geno said they were morons, but could handle stealing a couple dogs."

"Hey, watch it," Rooster's brother said. "Be careful about who you're calling a moron."

"And we did handle it," Coke Bottle said. "It was easy."

"You stole the wrong dogs, moron," the woman said.

"But they looked just like the dogs in the picture," Coke Bottle said.

"They're Golden Retrievers," the woman said. "They all look like the ones in the picture."

"Don't blame us, lady," Rooster's brother said. "They were right outside the store, just like he said they would be."

"Well, obviously it was two different dogs," the man said. "Didn't you bother to check?"

"Check what?" Coke Bottle said.

"To see if they'd been fixed," the woman said.

"Fixed? What was wrong with them?" Coke Bottle said.

"Wow," Josie whispered. "How did you manage to escape that gene pool, Rooster?"

"It wasn't easy," Rooster said.

"Fixed as in spayed or neutered, moron," the woman said.

"How would I know that?" Coke Bottle said.

"Let me grab a pair of scissors, and I'll show you," the woman said.

"Okay, let's calm down," the man said. "I guess we'll just have to figure out a different way to grab the dogs."

"Not using these two cretins, we won't," the woman said. "We'll do it ourselves."

"I'm not sure that's such a good idea," the man said. "What if somebody sees us?"

"Let me worry about that," the woman said. "We need to get out of here."

"Before you go," Rooster's brother said. "There's still the matter of payment."

"You stole the wrong dogs," the woman said. "Are you telling me you still expect to be paid?"

"That's exactly what I'm telling you, lady."

"Yeah, you hired us to steal two dogs, and that's exactly what we did," Coke Bottle said.

"I can't believe what I'm hearing," the woman said. "You know, if I had a gun, I think I might just shoot you."

"You mean a gun like this?" Rooster's brother said.

"Uh-oh," the man said. "Just put that down. There's no need for that."

"Well, would you look at that," the woman said. "Dumb and Dumber are carrying guns. They really need to do something about the gun laws in this country."

"That's enough, Sylvia," the man said. "Now how much was your fee again?"

"Two grand," Rooster's brother said."

"Yes, of course," the man said. "We'll just have to step outside and go to the car to get it."

"Nice try," Rooster's brother said. "Empty your pockets."

"I will not," the woman said.

"Lady, you aren't going to look very good with a hole in your forehead."

"Okay," Rooster whispered. "I've heard enough. You two stay here until I call you."

Rooster stepped out of the alcove and headed for the main living area of the camp.

"Uh-oh," Coke Bottle said.

"Rooster. What are you doing here?" his brother said.

"Drop the guns right now," Rooster said in a voice that made the hair on the back of my neck stand up.

Then we began a series of events that played out over the next thirty seconds that I would replay in my head at least a hundred times over the next few days.

We heard the clatter of the guns landing on the floor, glanced at each other and nodded, then raced into the room just as the lights went out. I took my first step in the darkness, tripped over what I assumed was a footstool and fell flat on my face.

Then I heard a blood-curdling scream.

The silence returned then I heard the front door opening and the footsteps of two people racing for the door. They ran directly into Chef Claire who was heading inside. All three bodies hit the floor, then two people clamored out the door, and I heard the sound of them running until it faded away.

"Suzy? Josie?" Chef Claire said.

"We're here," I said. "Are you okay?"

"Yeah, I'm fine. What's going on?"

"Stay tuned," I said. "Rooster?"

"Yeah."

"What are you doing?"

"I'm trying to get my hands on my idiot brother."

"Get out of here!" Coke Bottle screamed.

I heard the sound of someone running down a flight of stairs and the sound of a different door opening.

I climbed to my feet, took a few steps, then tripped over something else and reached out to catch myself. But the only thing I grabbed was air, and I started falling, then tumbling down a long set of stairs. I bounced several times then landed on a concrete floor. Seconds later, somebody else completed their journey down the stairs and landed right on top of me. Whatever air I had left in my lungs disappeared, and I groaned. I tried to extricate myself from the man lying on top of me but he wasn't moving, and I assumed that he'd been knocked out by the fall.

Something was pressing hard into my chest, and I grabbed the object and jerked it free. I rolled out from underneath the man and realized I was covered in a sticky substance that reminded me of melted chocolate. Still surrounded by total darkness, I climbed to my feet holding the object and stared around through the blackness. Then the lights came on, and I looked down at Rooster's brother who was staring up at me with a blank stare and a massive wound near his heart. Then I looked down at the large kitchen knife I was holding in my hand.

"Well, I'll be," said the person standing at the top of the stairs and staring down at me. "Are you getting all this, Jerry?"

"Oh, don't worry. I got all of it," Jerry the Cameraman said.

"Okay, on me," Jessica Talbot said. "This is Jessica Talbot, and I'm speaking to you from a remote hunting camp near Clay Bay, a place that is destined to become known as *The Small Town Murder Capital of the Country.*"

"That's good," Jerry said without looking up from the camera.

"Of course it's good," Jessica said, brushing the hair away from her eyes before continuing. "The person you see holding the bloody knife at the bottom of the stairs, a knife we can only assume is the murder weapon, is Suzy Chandler, a lifelong resident of Clay Bay. Only moments ago, an unidentified man was murdered, and his lifeless body is now sprawled at Ms. Chandler's feet. It's just a pity that we weren't able to get here a few minutes sooner. Now, we'll never know if we might have been able to save that poor man's life."

I stared up at her, then at the red light on the camera that was again focused squarely on me. I looked around the basement and caught a glimpse of my bloody face and clothes in a mirror, then dropped the knife, stunned.

Rooster, followed by Josie and Chef Claire, clamored down the stairs then carefully maneuvered themselves around the body.

"Are you okay?" Josie said.

"I think so," I said, slowly.

"She's in shock," Rooster said. "Suzy, sit down."

Rooster guided me to a chair, and I plopped down and stared around the room still dazed.

"Is he dead?" I whispered.

"Yeah, he is," Rooster said.

"I'm so sorry, Rooster. But I didn't kill him."

"I know you didn't, Suzy," Rooster said.

"Thank you for believing me," I whispered.

"She's out of it. We need to get her out of here," Josie said.

"No," I said. "I need to wait for Chief Abrams. This is a crime scene."

"Suzy, for once will you just listen to reason?" Josie said.

"I need to wait," I whispered, looking up at her.

"Unbelievable," Josie said. "Okay, we'll wait."

"Rooster?"

"Yes, Suzy?"

"Didn't you say there was some sort of tunnel connecting this camp with your other one about a quarter mile away?" I said, starting to regain some of my focus.

"Yes, there is," he said. "Why?"

"Because I bet that's where they're keeping Al and Dente," I said.

Chef Claire glanced around and spotted the door that was partially open. She looked at Rooster who nodded.

"That's it," he said. "There's a light switch just inside on the right."

Chef Claire and Josie managed to get the heavy door open. Josie turned the lights on, and she and Chef Claire disappeared down the tunnel. In the distance, I heard the sound of barking, and I smiled. A few minutes later, I heard happy whimpering as Chef Claire stepped out of the tunnel cradling Dente in her arms. Josie soon followed carrying Al who had his front paws wrapped around her shoulders and was nuzzling her neck, punctuated with a succession of affectionate licks.

"Well, look at that," Josie said. "I guess Al's finally forgiven me."

Chapter 10

By the time Chief Abrams arrived, I was sitting in the living area with a blanket wrapped around my shoulders sipping tea. I knew I probably looked like a little old granny sitting in her favorite chair, but I felt like I'd just gone ten rounds with a long flight of stairs and lost. I ached all over and was sure I had several cuts and bruises. But the rapidly congealing blood I was covered in was preventing me from doing a closer inspection.

Josie and Chef Claire were sitting on a couch still holding the dogs. Al and Dente, still basking in the glow of their recovery, had made it perfectly clear they weren't going anywhere. Rooster was slowly pacing back and forth, deep in thought. Jessica and Jerry were huddled in the kitchen area whispering excitedly. When Chief Abrams came through the front door, he headed straight for me.

"Not your best look, Suzy," Chief Abrams said. "Are you okay?"

"I'm fine," I said, nodding.

"Why don't you tell me what happened?" he said, grabbing a folding chair and sitting down across from me.

I started to recount the events, but Rooster held up a hand to stop me. He glared at the cameraman.

"Turn that thing off," Rooster said.

"Not likely, Bubba," Jerry the Cameraman said, glancing up from the eyepiece to grin at Rooster.

Rooster smiled and slowly walked toward Jerry. Then I heard a soft snap, and a thud as the camera fell to the floor.

"You broke my finger," Jerry said, clutching his hand.

"Lucky for you, you've got nine left," Rooster said.

"Chief. Arrest that man for assault," Jerry said.

"Uh, no," Chief Abrams said, glancing over his shoulder before refocusing on me. "Go ahead."

I recounted the events as I remembered them and he scribbled copious notes as I talked. When I finished, he patted my knee and walked down the stairs. A few minutes later, he returned and sat back down.

"Man, that's a lot of blood," Chief Abrams said. "Whoever put that knife in him either knew what to aim for, or he got very lucky." He glanced at Rooster. "I'm sorry for your loss, Rooster. I know you two weren't close, and that he had his problems, but still."

"Thanks, Chief. Given some of the choices he made, I'm surprised he lasted as long as he did," Rooster said, then glared at Jerry. "I said put that thing down."

"Don't let him intimidate you, Jerry," Jessica said.

"That's easy for you to say," Jerry said, setting the camera on the kitchen table. "It's not your fingers he's breaking."

"Chief, if it's okay with you," Jessica said, turning sweet. "Jerry and I need to get going."

"I'm sorry Ms. Talbot," Chief Abrams said. "But I'm going to need statements from both of you before I can let you leave."

"With all due respect, Chief," Jessica said, "I must say-"

"You know, Ms. Talbot," Chief said, cutting her off. "One thing I've learned over the years is that when somebody starts a sentence by saying with all due respect, it means they don't have any for the person they're talking to."

"Yeah, that's very interesting, Chief Abrams," Jessica said, flashing him a quick smile. "I'll try to remember that. But as I was about to say before you rudely interrupted me is that Jerry and I need to do some editing and get this story submitted in time for the eleven o'clock news."

"With all due respect, Ms. Talbot," Chief Abrams said, returning her smile. "That's not gonna happen."

"Of course it is," Jessica said, glaring at him. "This story will go viral within an hour after it runs."

"Yeah, it probably would," he said, nodding. "Which sounds like another good reason why you're not going to run it. At least the video anyway."

"But the video is the whole story," Jessica said.

"Yeah, funny how that works," Chief Abrams said, smiling. "Whatever happened to the written word?"

"Not only don't you not have the right to stop me from using the story," Jessica said. "You don't have the ability."

"Not only don't you not? Do your lawyers encourage you to speak in double negatives?" Josie said, frowning. "Jessica, I know you're a little rattled at the moment, but surely you can do better that."

"Who asked for your input?" Jessica said, glaring at Josie.

"Hey, if I waited for people to ask, I'd never get a word in," Josie deadpanned.

"Before I forget, Jerry," Chief Abrams said. "I'm going to need to take that camera with me."

"That's highly unlikely," Jessica said. "That camera is the property of my employer."

"It also contains possible evidence about a murder," Chief Abrams said.

Jerry nodded and inched his way closer to the kitchen table. He casually placed a hand on the back of the camera.

"Jerry," Rooster said, his voice barely above a whisper. "If you try to remove the memory card from that camera, you're going to lose a lot more than a finger."

Jerry took a step back, and Rooster grabbed the camera off the table and tossed it onto an empty chair. Jerry looked at Jessica and shrugged.

"This is unbelievable," Jessica said. "Incompetent and corrupt. What a delightful combination for a police chief to have."

"You need to watch yourself, Ms. Talbot," Chief Abrams said.

"What I'd like to watch is you arresting somebody," she snapped.

"You know, I am thinking about doing that," he said. "I thought I'd start with you and Jerry here."

"What an absurd idea," Jessica said.

"No, let's hear him out," Josie said, leaning forward.

"I can't wait to get out of this hick town," she said. "Okay, I'll play. What are the so-called charges?"

"I thought I'd start with the willful tampering of a crime scene and threatening a police officer."

"What?" Jessica said. "It's no wonder people are dropping like flies in this town."

"Don't forget trespassing and breaking and entering, Chief," Rooster said.

"Thanks, Rooster. I forgot those two," Chief Abrams said, beaming at him. "I assume you want to press charges?"

"I do."

"Okay, okay. I got it," Jessica said, sitting down at the kitchen table. "You win. You might as well sit down and relax Jerry. Deputy Fife is obviously going to keep us here for a while. But this isn't over."

"No, it's not," Josie said. "You still have a dog show to cover."

"Ah, crap. I forgot all about that," Jessica said, rubbing her forehead then glancing up at the ceiling. "Get me to New York, please."

"If you're looking for spiritual intervention, I think you're looking in the wrong direction, Jessica," Josie said, pointing down at the floor.

We heard a knock on the front door and Freddie, our local medical examiner, stepped inside trailed by two paramedics pushing a stretcher.

"Hi, folks," Freddie said, glancing around then settling on me. "Are you okay, Suzy?"

"Hey, Freddie," I said. "I'm fine."

"I take it that's not your blood," Freddie said.

"No, it's not mine."

"Good," he said, placing a hand on my shoulder. "Where's the body?"

Chief Abrams pointed at the stairs.

"Go ahead and have a look," Chief Abrams said. "But don't move the body before the state police get here." He glanced at the two paramedics. "Sorry, guys, but I'm going to have to ask you two to wait outside for now."

The paramedics nodded and headed for the door, but left the stretcher behind. Freddie headed downstairs, and Chief Abrams stood and looked around the room.

"So, this man and woman left through the front door just after the lights went out?"

"I think so," I said, glancing at Chef Claire and Josie. "Right?"

"Yeah, I think so," Josie said. "But it all happened so fast."

"Do you think they had time to stab Rooster's brother?" Chief Abrams said.

I thought hard for a moment, then looked around at my friends. All three of them seemed to be pondering the question as well.

"I think so," Rooster said, eventually.

"Me too," Josie said.

"And your cousin?" Chief Abrams said.

"I can't believe it, but I completely forgot all about him," Rooster said, glancing around.

"Do you think he could have gone out one of the back doors?" Chief Abrams said.

"I guess it's possible," Rooster said. "It's was dark and pretty hectic for a while."

I had forgotten about Coke Bottle as well. Then I remembered hearing the sound of someone running down the stairs.

"I think he went downstairs," I said. "And the door leading to the tunnel was partially open."

"He probably used the tunnel to get over to the other hunting camp," Rooster said.

"Is there an access road over there he could drive out of?" Chief Abrams said.

"Yeah, there is. It's pretty overgrown, but if you know your way around, it's not a problem."

"Do you know what kind of car he has?" Chief Abrams said.

"No, I wouldn't have a clue. I haven't seen either one of them in about a year," Rooster said.

"Well, he hasn't gone far yet," Chief Abrams said. "We'll get some roadblocks set up as soon as I find some cell coverage."

"I'm sure Coke Bottle hasn't gone very far at all," Josie said.

We all looked at her and followed her eyes to the top of the stairs. A pair of thick-lensed glasses was sitting on the floor.

"You think your cousin carried a spare set of glasses?" I said.

"I seriously doubt it," Rooster said, shaking his head. "That would require common sense and a bit of foresight."

"He wouldn't try driving a car without his glasses, would he?"

"You've met the man, Suzy," Rooster said. "What do you think?"

Chief Abrams scribbled a note on his pad and then focused his attention on Jessica and Jerry.

"You two feel like explaining how you just happened to show up here?" Chief Abrams said.

"No," Jessica said.

"Okay," Chief Abrams said, jotting down another note.

"What did you just write down?" Jerry said, massaging his hand.

"Oh, that's nothing. I just added accessory to murder as another potential charge."

Jessica snorted. She noticed Jerry staring at her.

"Relax, Jerry. He's just trying to scare you."

"Well, it's working, Jessica," Jerry said, then turned to Chief Abrams. "We followed them from the restaurant."

"Black SUV with tinted windows, right?" Chef Claire said, stroking Dente's head. "We thought it was a government car."

"Most people do," Jessica said. "That's why I bought it."

"Why did you follow us?" I said.

"I saw you huddling at the restaurant like a gang of conspirators and figured something was up. And since we were done at the restaurant, we had the rest of the afternoon free," Jessica said, shrugging. "It looks like my journalistic instincts were right again."

Josie snorted.

"And you just decided to let yourself in?" Chief Abrams said.

Jessica sighed loudly.

"Yes, we were approaching the house, and we heard people talking. Then the lights went out, and we heard a scream. In my business, that means breaking news."

"Did you see two people running out the front door on your way in?" Chief Abrams said.

"No, but we heard them," Jerry said. "I think they headed for the woods."

"This entire area is in the woods, idiot," Rooster said. "That's why I built it here."

"For the peace and quiet?" Jessica said.

"Yes."

"Well, judging from today's events, I guess that didn't work out too well, did it?" Jessica said, smiling.

Then we were all startled by a loud crash outside the back of the camp. Rooster frowned, then shook his head. Al and Dente worked their way even closer to Chef Claire and Josie.

"It's okay, guys," Chef Claire whispered.

"What the heck was that?" Chief Abrams said, his hand on his holster.

"Take a wild guess," Rooster said. "Toss me that flashlight, Josie."

Rooster opened the door we'd come through earlier and stood at the top of steps shining the flashlight outside into the darkness.

"Unbelievable," Rooster said, staring out. "How the heck did he manage to do that?"

"Your cousin drove into a tree, didn't he?" Chief Abrams said.

"Yup, he sure did."

"Is he hurt?" Chief Abrams said.

"It doesn't look like it, but give me a minute," Rooster said. "You want him cuffed?"

"Yeah, it's probably not a bad idea," Chief Abrams said, tossing a pair of handcuffs across the room.

"I'll be right back," Rooster said, then headed down the stairs.

We listened to their muffled exchange, then heard Coke Bottle cry out in pain a couple of times. Then Rooster walked back inside massaging his hand.

"He's cuffed to the steering wheel," he said to Chief Abrams.

"Thanks. I'll deal with him later."

"I knew I should have brought Titan," Rooster said, still massaging his hand.

"Who's Titan?" Jerry said.

"My German shepherd," Rooster said.

"Does he bite?" Jerry said.

"Only when I tell him to."

"Can I go get cleaned up, Chief?" I said.

"Sure. Go ahead," he said, nodding.

"You'll find some clothes in the big bedroom."

"I doubt if any of your clothes are going to fit me, Rooster."

"No, there are some women's clothes in there," he said.

"Really?"

"Hey, I have a personal life."

"So I'm beginning to discover," I said, getting up out of my chair and walking toward the bathroom.

"You're just going to let her wander off by herself?" Jessica said.

"Sure. Why wouldn't I?"

"Well, I just thought that someone who earlier today said that she'd love to bury a kitchen knife in the chest of the person who stole those dogs would be a woman you'd want to keep a close eye on."

I stopped and glared at her across the room. Jerry was staring down at the floor, but Jessica gave me her best fake smile. Luckily for her, I wasn't within reach of any cutlery. Then I noticed Chief Abrams giving me a strange look.

"If you don't believe me," Jessica said. "Just check the tape."

Chapter 11

I took a sip of wine, then winced and glared at Josie.

"Hey, take it easy, Thumbelina," I snapped. "That hurts."

"Don't be such a baby," Josie said.

After we'd gotten home, I'd discovered a large splinter buried deep in the back of my shoulder. Rather than finish my Thanksgiving with a trip to the emergency room, I'd asked Josie to get it out. Now her patience was wearing as thin as my tolerance for pain. But the scalpel and tweezers she was using to dig the object out had momentarily taken my mind off the bumps and bruises I'd sustained falling down the stairs.

"Hang on," I said, draining my wine glass and holding it out for Chef Claire to refill.

"Okay, that's all of the splinters," Josie said, setting the tweezers down on a small metal tray. "But I had to cut you to get them all out."

"No kidding."

Josie laughed.

"You're going to need a few stitches," she said. "But be a good girl, and you'll get a lollipop when we're done."

"Thanks, but I think I'll stick with the wine."

"I didn't think vets were supposed to work on people," Chief Abrams said.

"We're not," she said, continuing her work without looking up. "You going to arrest me, Chief?"

"Actually, I thought I might ask you to take a look at one of the cuts I got walking through those woods."

"Okay, it's ready to go," Sammy said. "When you're ready, just push the play button on the camera, and it'll show on the TV."

"Thanks, Sammy," I said.

"No problem. I need to head down to the Inn. Jill and I are doing inventory tonight."

"Swing by later," Chef Claire said. "I'm reheating some leftover lasagna. But don't wait too long, I'm pretty sure Josie worked up quite an appetite today."

"Funny," Josie said, tugging one of the stitches tight.

"Ow. Hey, she said it. Don't take it out on me," I said, glancing over my shoulder.

"Yeah, but you were thinking it," Josie said. "Okay, we're done here. Just let me get a bandage on it."

"Thanks," I said, taking a large sip of wine.

"Let's check out this footage before dinner," Chief Abrams said.

"Good idea," Chef Claire said, rubbing Al and Dente's heads who were nestled next to her on the couch. "I can't believe you threatened to kill the dognappers."

"It wasn't like that at all," I said. "It was only a smart part of a casual conversation I was having with Alexandra. We could have just as easily been talking about the weather."

"If it gets much colder, I'm going to stab somebody in the chest?" Josie deadpanned.

"Josie, please," my mother said.

"Sorry, Mrs. C."

"I should hope so," she said, then looked at me. "Darling, how many times do I have to remind you that everything you say these days has a good chance of being recorded?"

"Obviously at least one more time than you did, Mom," I said, grabbing the remote.

We watched in silence as the restaurant footage began to play. Several close-up snippets of Jessica beaming into the camera and delivering homey platitudes randomly appeared in between shots of people eating and laughing. It was the raw feed of the day's events, but I knew that an editor could quickly cut the video together into a coherent story. Despite my deep loathing for the woman, I had to admit that she was very good at what she did.

Then I saw myself chatting with Alexandra and heard my comment about what I'd like to do to the dognappers. I cringed and downed the rest of my wine.

"Not good," I said.

"No, it's not. Especially when it's combined with the shot of you standing at the bottom of the stairs covered in blood and holding the knife," Chief Abrams said. "But as long as it doesn't ever make it on the air, you'll be fine."

"So, you can bury it?" my mother said.

"Well, I can use the murder evidence argument to stall for a while," Chief Abrams said.

"For how long?" my mother said.

"Probably a couple of days," he said. "Maybe a week. But that network has a lot of lawyers whose job it is to deal with things like this. And when it comes to stories that promise big ratings, they fight pretty hard."

"I'll talk to Bob," my mother said.

"Do you think he'll listen to you?" I said.

"Yes. But only up to a point, darling. He still has his own corporate masters he needs to keep happy."

"Two human interest stories, plus an on the spot report from a murder scene," Josie said, shaking her head. "That's a big score for Jessica."

"Indeed," my mother said. "Don't worry, darling. We'll figure something out."

"We better," Josie deadpanned. "You look dreadful in orange."

"You're such a big help," I said, punching her on the shoulder.

"Relax," Josie said. "You didn't kill the guy. The worst thing that can happen is your reputation gets permanently damaged."

"And that's supposed to make me feel better?"

"Hey, I said it was the *worst* thing that could happen. But it's not going to," Josie said. "We'll figure something out."

"Has Coke Bottle started talking yet?" I said.

"Not much. The state police took him into custody when he was at the emergency room," Chief Abrams said. "He said it wasn't his idea to steal the dogs and that Rooster's brother threatened him if he didn't go along with it."

"What about the man and woman?" I said.

"Coke Bottle said he never got their names, but he does remember the man calling her Sylvia a couple of times."

"I heard him call her that," I said, nodding. "Did he give you a description?"

"Yeah," Chief Abrams said, laughing. "I'm currently on the lookout for two blurry, vaguely-shaped individuals. Just my luck that our only eyewitness is blind as a bat."

"You were saying earlier that they stole the wrong dogs," my mother said.

"Yeah, they did," I said. "They must have been trying to steal Alexandra's two Goldens. And since they're Al and Dente's parents, it would be an easy mistake to make."

"Especially for a couple of idiots like those two," Josie said.

"By the way, I called Alexandra and gave her an update. She was wondering if she could keep Lucky and Lucy at the Inn while she's judging the dog show. When I told her we heard the man and woman say that they were just going to have to handle it by themselves, she got nervous. And she doesn't want to take any chances."

"That's probably a good idea," Josie said. "Who's scheduled to work on Saturday?"

"Tommy," I said. "But I thought we might ask Sammy if he wants to work a little overtime and help him out."

"Yeah. Good idea. Let's do that," Josie said.

"And I'll be at the show along with several state police in street clothes," Chief Abrams said. "You really think they're going to be there?"

"I do," I said, nodding. "Especially if they're assuming that Alexandra is planning on bringing her Goldens."

"It makes sense," Chief Abrams said. "She said she takes them everywhere with her."

"Are Alexandra's dogs that valuable?" my mother said.

"Did you ever see the commercial of the two Goldens running through the water wearing diamonds?"

"Of course, diamonds always get my attention, darling."

"That's them. And the dogs have their own calendar, tee shirts, coffee mugs, you name it. And I heard that Alexandra's in negotiations to get them their own line of dog food."

"Really?" Josie said, glancing down at her Newfie who was sprawled out across her feet. "Did you hear that, Captain? Do you see what's possible when you simply apply yourself?"

I laughed when Captain opened his eyes and raised his head a few inches off the floor to glance at Josie, then thumped his tail and went back to sleep.

"Her Goldens are a big deal in the dog world," I said.

"And probably the envy of every other dog breeder?" Chief Abrams said, raising an eyebrow.

"Now that is a very interesting idea, Chief," I said.

"All I know is that their puppies cost a small fortune," Chef Claire said, patting both dogs. "Freddie and Jackson said they each spent three thousand for these guys,"

"Wow," my mother said. "That's a lot of money for a dog." She glanced at us and shrugged. "No offense."

"But worth every penny," Josie said, reaching over to rub Al's head.

"How many puppies are in a litter?" my mother said.

"Goldens?" Josie said. "Usually somewhere between six and ten."

"One litter a year?" my mother said.

"I wouldn't recommend any more often than that," Josie said. "But the people running these scams don't give a squat about the dogs. And they'll try to push the females to have two litters a year. But it's really hard on them."

"At three grand a pop, that's a pretty good chunk of change," Chief Abrams said.

"Especially if they've got a dozen or so females pushing out litters," I said.

"But what about the pedigree and lineage papers you're always talking about?" my mother said. "That's a pretty big deal for people spending all that money, right?"

"If you have access to some of the databases that are out there, it's actually pretty easy to fake them," Josie said. "Give me a couple of hours, and I could probably convince you that Suzy is a direct descendant of the Queen of England."

"Not with those table manners you couldn't," my mother said, laughing.

"Funny, Mom."

"Good one, Mrs. C.," Josie said, laughing.

"Thank you, dear. It's nice to see that somebody gets me," my mother said, standing up. "Okay, I need to run to a meeting. What's my share for today's dinner?"

"Don't worry about it, Mom. We're going to pay for it out of the restaurant."

"Won't that kill your profits this month?" she said, glancing around at the three of us.

Chef Claire, Josie, and I looked at each other and shrugged it off.

"Not enough to worry about, Mom."

"We're having a good year," Chef Claire said, refilling all our wine glasses.

"Okay, but I insist on paying next year," she said, waving as she headed for the kitchen door.

When we heard her car roar out of the driveway, Josie glanced over at me.

"It's nice to see that she's not still mad at you," she said.

"Oh, she's still mad," I said. "She's just waiting until we're alone before she lets me have it."

"So, you're going to be traveling in small groups for the foreseeable future," Josie said.

"Exactly," I said, gently setting Chloe down on the floor and getting up out of my chair. "Judging by the smells coming from the kitchen, I'm betting that the lasagna is ready."

"I think you're right," Chef Claire said. "Would you like to stay for dinner, Chief?"

"I was so hoping you'd ask," he said. "I hate to go to an empty house on an empty stomach. The wife and the dog drove to Pennsylvania to see the kids."

"You're all alone at Thanksgiving?" I said.

"Well, let's see. Earlier today I had dinner with over a hundred of my closest friends, then spent several hours dealing with a murder and tramping through the woods. And now I'm here watching home movies with you guys. Trust me, by the time I get home later, I'll be more than happy with a little alone time."

"Good point," I said. "And I'm glad you're sticking around for dinner. Maybe you'll have a few ideas about how we can push a few of Jessica's buttons at the dog show."

"You're not thinking about getting even with her by breaking the law, are you?"

"Of course not," I said. "Why would you ask me a question like that?"

"I just wanted to know if I needed to be looking the other way when you did," he said, winking at me. "You know, as much of a fan as I am of Chef Claire's lasagna, shouldn't we be eating turkey sandwiches tonight?"

"That's my fault," Chef Claire said. "I was in so much of a hurry to start looking for Al and Dente I completely forgot to bring some leftovers home."

"So we're stuck with lasagna?" Josie deadpanned.

"Yeah."

"Oh, no. Not the briar patch."

Chapter 12

Alexandra slowly made her way through the condo area, spending as much time with our beloved mutts as she did with the purebreds. Because of that, my estimation of her went up several notches. She was what Josie and I liked to call an equal opportunity dog person. She reached into one of the condos to pet the gorgeous Beagle-Pitbull mix we'd found abandoned a few months ago. Alexandra stood and took another look around.

"And you take every dog in?" she said.

"We try to," Josie said. "But occasionally we have to say no because we're completely full."

"And you have a strict no-kill policy?" Alexandra said.

"Absolutely," I said.

"And if you're at full capacity, but come across a dog about to be put down?" she said.

"We find room," Josie said, shrugging.

"You're doing wonderful work here," she said, bending over to pet Tiny, our massive Great Dane.

"We like to think so," Josie said. "And just so you don't worry about Lucky and Lucy, all our dogs are up to date on all their vaccinations, and we've never had a single case of kennel cough or anything else that could be passed from dog to dog."

"That doesn't surprise me," she said. "You could eat off these floors."

"Let's not get carried away, Alexandra," Josie said. "Even I have my limits."

"Unless she drops her sandwich," I said.

"Funny."

"I really don't want to leave them overnight," Alexandra said.

"Not a problem," I said. "Just drop them off tomorrow morning on your way to the show. We open at seven."

"Perfect," she said. "I'm thinking about staying for a few days after the show. I hate going home to an empty house."

"When is your husband getting back?" I said.

"Wednesday," Alexandra said, reaching into her purse and holding up a family picture. "That's the family. My son followed in his father's footsteps and became a lawyer. My daughter wanted to be a vet, but she couldn't get in and had to settle for medical school."

"Getting into vet school is tough," Josie said. "It took me two tries."

"Good looking kids. Your husband's a lawyer?" I said, looking at the photo of Alexandra's family with her two prize Goldens sitting and smiling for the camera.

"By training, yes. Now he handles most of the business side of our company. He's more comfortable hanging around with other lawyers, and I much prefer the company of dogs. It's an arrangement that works well for us."

I caught Josie's eye, and she gave me a small shake of her head telling me to let Alexandra's last statement pass without comment.

"I'll need to get home sometime on Tuesday at the latest," Alexandra said as we headed back toward the reception area. "Lucky has a freezing session scheduled."

We stepped inside reception and found Chef Claire and Sammy and Jill laughing as they watched the four Golden Retrievers roughhousing on the floor.

"You said Lucky has a freezing session?" Josie said, frowning.

"Actually, he has several coming up in the next few weeks," Alexandra said, smiling as she watched the dogs. "I need to help the clinic get restocked."

"I'm sorry, Alexandra," I said. "But I think we're going to need a little clarification."

"Of course. That must have sounded strange," she said, giving us a small smile. "Ever since Lucky and Lucy started to get successful, I've been freezing Lucky's sperm. Do you have any idea what that's worth?"

"Well, I'm no expert on dog semen," Josie said. "But I could probably ballpark it."

"It's quite a lot of money," Alexandra said. "Harold suggested that we *bank* as much of it as we could, so we've been taking Lucky to the clinic on a weekly basis for the past few years. Does that make me a money-grubbing monster?"

"Well, I can't speak to that, Alexandra," Josie deadpanned. "But I'm sure it makes Lucky a pretty happy dog."

"Yes," she said, giggling and lowering her voice to a whisper. "If I even mention the word *clinic* these days, Lucky heads straight for the car."

Lucky paused from his play session, cocked his head, and looked at Alexandra. Then he resumed his playful attack on one of Dente's front paws.

"But last week, I got a call from the owner of the clin-, you know what, and he told me they'd been robbed. Their entire inventory was stolen."

I glanced at Josie who was already pondering the implications of what Alexandra had just told us.

"So, we're going to be rapidly restocking Lucky's supply," Alexandra said, then caught our expressions. "What?"

"I'm just wondering if the robbery at the sperm bank and the threat of someone kidnapping your dogs could be connected," I said.

Alexandra frowned and looked off into the distance.

"I suppose it's possible," she said, shaking her head. "I hate those people."

"The people that trade in black market dogs?" I said.

"Yes. Them and even some who call themselves legitimate breeders," she said.

111

"Are there a lot of people who are envious of your success, Alexandra?" I said.

"Of course. I've learned that envy seems to be an integral part of basic human nature."

"Another good reason to spend as much time as you can surrounded by dogs," Josie said.

"Exactly," Alexandra said, staring off into the distance, her eyes dark, her lips pursed.

"Will any of them be here for the dog show tomorrow?" Josie said.

"Yes, several. You met a few of them at your restaurant yesterday," she said. "But I doubt if their envy would extend to dognapping. Or robbery."

"Maybe," I said. "But let's keep a close eye on things tomorrow."

"And you're sure that Lucky and Lucy will be safe here?" Alexandra said.

"They will," Josie said, nodding.

"Thank you. I don't know what I'd do if anything ever happened to them," Alexandra said, glancing down at her watch. "I have to stop by the venue for a walkthrough, but I'll see you tomorrow."

"Looking forward to it," I said.

Alexandra opened the front door then paused and looked back at us.

"You're absolutely sure they'll be safe here?" she said.

112

"Yes, you have our word," I said. "And if you hear any more about the robbery, please let us know."

"I'll ask the owner of the clinic when I see him on Tuesday."

Lucky clamored to his feet and made a beeline for the door. Alexandra shook her head as we roared with laughter.

"Now I've done it," she said. "Lucy. Let's go, girl. Time to hit the road."

We watched the female Golden trot gracefully toward the door and wait for Alexandra's instructions. Then the two of them strolled toward the car where Lucky was impatiently pacing back and forth.

"Typical male," I said.

"I guess we can't blame him," Josie said. "If you had a weekly appointment like that, we'd never get you out of the car."

"You're really not funny."

"Disagree."

Chapter 13

Remembering our upcoming trip to Grand Cayman where I'd be forced to put my pasty-white winter complexion and a whole lot of skin on full display, I went easy on the stuffing and settled for a double helping of leftover turkey. I settled into the chair next to Rooster at the chef table in the kitchen and waited until Chef Claire joined us.

The restaurant was closed, and since all the food from yesterday's feast was here, rather than cart it all home, we decided to just eat lunch here. Josie was chatting casually with Chief Abrams and Chef Claire started feeding small pieces of turkey to Al and Dente who were sprawled at her feet.

"You're not going to let them out of your sight for a while, are you?" I said, laughing.

"Not a chance," she said. "No, that's enough for now, Al."

Al emitted what sounded like a low grumble, but settled right down and closed his eyes.

"Good dogs," Rooster said, glancing down at them.

"Any word from your cousin?" I said, starting to work my way through a slice of white meat.

"I swung by the state police station this morning, which, as you know, is something I enjoy about as much as swimming in the

River in December," Rooster said, taking a sip of his mimosa. "At first, he didn't feel like talking."

"But you convinced him eventually," I said.

"I did. I told him that now that my brother was gone, he was about the only family I've got left."

"And cousin Walter saw dollar signs flashing before his eyes?" I said.

"He certainly did. That was something he was able to see very clearly. He has no idea how much money I've got, but as soon as he got an inkling he might inherit it, he got very chatty."

"What are you going to do with all your money, Rooster?"

"Start spending heavy near the end, then I thought I might leave what's left to you," he said, casually chewing.

"I don't need your money, Rooster," I said, shaking my head. "I don't know what to do with what I have now."

"Judging by the condition of that contraption you drive, that's pretty clear. The money wouldn't be for you. It would be for the dogs. What do you think?"

"I think you should spend every last dollar and make sure your last check bounces," I said, patting his hand.

"Now that would be the perfect way for someone like me to go out," he said, giving the idea some serious consideration.

"So, you wouldn't consider leaving it to Coke Bottle?"

"Not a chance. I can't even count how much money I've given him and my dead brother over the years," he said, frowning. "He'll be lucky if he gets invited to my funeral."

"What did he have to say?"

"Other than saying he was sorry for driving my car into a tree?"

"That was your car?"

"It was one of them. They stole it out of the garage I use to store old boats and cars."

"I guess I can't blame you for cutting him out of the will," I said, shaking my head. "I can't believe your own family would steal from you."

"It wasn't the first time. Anyway, Walter said that the man didn't say much the whole time they were in the camp. But the woman was pretty chatty. She mentioned her place in Colorado a couple of times. But she was very cranky with the guy the whole time they were there. And it sounded to my cousin like they were a couple. You know, of the horizontal variety."

"Got it," I said. "Does he know which one of them killed Jerry?"

"He's pretty sure it was the woman. Apparently, she was in the kitchen just before the lights went out."

"And she grabbed the knife and headed across the room?" I said, trying to recreate the scene in my head.

"Yeah, that's what he thinks happened," Rooster said. "Then he told me that he thought the woman was actually planning to stab the guy instead of my brother."

"Now that's interesting," I said, raising an eyebrow.

"Yeah, I thought that might get your motor running," he said, laughing.

"Did Walter hear them talking about dogs?"

"Yeah, he did. But my cousin's ability to process information, like his eyesight, is pretty limited. He said they talked about needing to get their supply restocked," Rooster said, frowning. "Does that make any sense to you?"

"Maybe. I think we might be dealing with another black market scam involving dogs. The supply they were referring to was probably dog semen."

"Hey, we're trying to eat here," Josie said. "New topic, please."

"The things people are willing to do for a buck," Rooster said, softly. "And you think they might take another shot at that dog judge's Goldens?"

"Yeah. And thanks again for agreeing to keep an eye on the Inn while we're at the dog show. Sammy and Tommy will be there, but we'll feel a lot more comfortable knowing you're there."

"I'm happy to do it. Now that tourist season is over, I'm worried that Titan might be losing his edge. I can't think of a better way to get it back than by him gnawing on some dognapper's leg."

"I hope it doesn't come to that, but if it does, I hope Titan is hungry," I said. "Did you get a chance to catch up with your ex-wife yet?"

"Yeah, we talked last night," he said, staring down at his plate before glancing over at me. "Aren't you going to ask how it went?"

"No, I don't think I am. If you want to tell me, you will."

"You're a smart woman, Suzy. You seem to know when to push and when to back off."

"Thanks. I think I get that from my father."

"Yeah, probably. Your mom doesn't seem to have much of a pause button."

"Do you?"

"Do I want to tell you how it went?"

"Yes."

"Back off," he said, then laughed.

"But she's doing okay, right?"

"She's fine. And she's got the most beautiful Springer Spaniel I've ever seen."

"I take it meeting the dog was the highlight of the evening."

"Without a doubt."

Chapter 14

When my mother and the town council first came up with the idea to hold a dog show, they'd asked Josie and me to serve on the planning committee. By the time our initial five-hour committee meeting finished, most members of the council were beginning to regret their decision to hold the show in the first place. The logistics were enormous and started with locating a dog group that was a member of the American Kennel Club to sanction the show.

When my mother wondered out loud why we even needed to bother, we explained to her that, if we wanted to award accredited championship points to the winning dogs, the show needed to be AKC sanctioned. After twenty minutes of questions and debate about what championship points were, and why they were important to the people and their dogs who participated, we finally moved on to the next item on the agenda.

The first item had turned out to be one of the easiest to cross off the list.

When the meeting finally adjourned, several members of the council remained sitting around the conference table staring forlornly at the to-do list we'd captured on a whiteboard. While they were trying to recover, my mother hit us up to be the primary sponsor of the show. Worn out from the meeting, we quickly agreed and wrote her a check on the spot.

She beamed at us and headed back to the conference room.

Josie and I headed home for wine and Advil.

But the committee eventually muddled its way through, and we'd ended up with what appeared to be a strong and manageable show that could probably be repeated annually. Big dog shows regularly have over a thousand dogs participating, and the dogs come from dozens of different breeds that are divided into seven separate groups. At first, my mother had grand designs to go big, but since we were holding the show at Clay Bay's multi-purpose arena that only held two thousand people, she'd scaled back when Josie asked her a very simple question.

"Where do you plan to put all the dogs?" Mrs. C.

In her desire to recreate a show like the big ones on TV, my mother had forgotten that while the one dog she was watching on the screen was being put through its paces, there were hundreds of other dogs waiting for their turn.

And they had to wait somewhere.

In the end, we'd reserved one side of the arena that included walkways and open spaces under the seating areas above. And since there was no way we could handle all seven sanctioned groups, we'd eventually decided on to limit our show to only the Sporting Group and cap entries at two-hundred. Since dogs from this group were often owned by local residents and extremely popular, the committee unanimously agreed that the Sporting Group would attract the most entries and sell the most tickets. They'd been right on both counts, and the event was sold out.

We got Chloe and Captain into my SUV, and by the time we got to the arena at eight in the morning, people and their dogs were everywhere. We'd rolled the dice on the weather and had gotten lucky. Partially cloudy and fifty degrees was downright balmy in late November in the Islands and the potential problem of how we'd handle wet and muddy dogs disappeared.

Inside, the registration area was busy, as was the section of the foyer we'd reserved for our adoption program. Jill was studying the results of her work and the dozen dogs that were resting comfortably inside the portable fencing she'd set up. She was chatting with three high school girls who worked for us during the summer and had volunteered to help out.

"Hey, guys," Jill said, kneeling down to rub Chloe and Captain's heads. "We just got set up, and we've already had two adoptions."

"That's great," I said. "Which ones?"

"The Cocker and the Lab-Retriever mix. I figured that since it was a Sporting Group show, it probably wouldn't be a bad idea to bring dogs from those breeds."

"Good call," Josie said. "Have you seen Alexandra?"

"She got here a few minutes ago. She said she was heading to her office," Jill said, laughing. "That is if a converted supply closet can actually be called an office."

"Yeah, we kind of ran out of room," I said, glancing around and waving to some friends. "Is she okay with the space?"

"Well, she said she'd seen much worse, so I think she is," Jill said. "She's a very nice woman."

"Yes, she is," I said.

"And fully recovered from her initial encounter with Rooster," Josie said.

I laughed. When Alexandra had stopped by earlier to drop off her dogs, Rooster was already there. He was wearing his usual attire right down to the boots without laces or socks. And if the grease-stained jeans and Grateful Dead tee shirt he was wearing hadn't raised her blood pressure a tick, then his unshaven face and the sweat-stained bandana on his head certainly did the trick. But after spending ten minutes with him, she'd relaxed, and by the time she was ready to leave for the show, they were chatting like old friends.

Josie and I walked into the arena and looked around. The decorating committee had done a great job, and they'd asked Sammy, one of Clay Bay's music aficionados, to put together a playlist for the show. He'd stayed with the dog theme, and we heard the end of John Hiatt's *My Dog and Me* transition seamlessly into Bowie's *Diamond Dogs*.

The hockey boards that were up most of the time in winter were gone, and the ice had been covered with its protective mat and wooden floor. On top of the floor was a bright green indoor-outdoor carpet that stretched the length of the rink and really popped. We nodded our approval as we walked toward the center ice area then walked down the small incline between two sections of seats. We found Alexandra studying the registration list inside the cramped confines of the converted closet.

"This is a strong field," she said, looking up from the list. "Should be a great show."

"Any early favorites jumping off the page?" Josie said, looking over Alexandra's shoulder.

"Well, I hate to pre-judge," she said, smiling. "But Glen and Abby Wilson's Chesapeake Bay Retriever always shows very well."

I remembered meeting the couple at Thanksgiving dinner as well as the tension between Abby and Alexandra. But if Alexandra was already saying good things about their dog, she didn't appear to be someone who held grudges. At least against dogs.

"And wait until you see Margaret Jenkins' Springer Spaniel. Magnificent dog," she said. "Maybe next year you can figure out a way to include the Working and Herding groups. Your Aussie Shepherd and the Newfie would both show very well."

"Thanks, Alexandra," I said, glancing at Josie. "But we really don't have much interest in showing our dogs."

"Yeah, we kind of like to let them set their own agenda if you know what I mean," Josie said.

"I understand completely," she said, stroking Chloe's fur. "And they deserve to be as spoiled as you want. Getting dogs show-ready is a lot of work and isn't for everybody." She clapped her hands and stood. "Okay, let's go look at some dogs."

She waved as she headed toward the show area.

"She's a very happy woman," Josie said, watching her walk away. "I think her life is a lot like ours."

"Then she's lucky," I said, glancing around the cramped space. "We should have done a better job finding a space for her to do her work and relax."

"Well, unless you want to put her in one of the women's bathrooms or on the roof, good luck."

I glanced up through the open ceiling at the boxes and spare lights that were stacked on the catwalk above the closet.

"Yeah, I know," I said. "But next year we have to do a better job."

"Let's say we get through today first, huh?"

"Okay," I said, clapping my hands. "Let's go find some dognappers."

"Sounds good. Right after we find Jessica and do your interview," she said, laughing.

"Ah, crap. I completely forgot."

"Relax. I think it's going to be a lot of fun," she said, grinning at me.

Jessica was easy to find. She was fake-smiling her way around the reception area, greeting well-wishers and signing the occasional autograph. She spotted us and nodded at Jerry the Cameraman to follow her as she headed our way.

"Good morning, ladies," Jessica said. "How are you doing, Slasher? Am I safe here, or are you packing cutlery?"

"Doesn't walking around with that smile hurt your face?" I said.

"After a while, yeah," Jessica said. "But as soon as I saw the two of you, problem solved, right?"

"Let's get this over with."

"I want that tape," Jessica said.

"And I want to be able to eat all the ice cream I want without gaining a pound," I said, flashing her a quick smile. "Life sucks, huh?"

"You won't be able to get within a thousand yards of a dog by the time I finish with you," she said, then turned to Jerry. "Let's find a quiet spot inside. But not anywhere near that hideous green carpet." Then she glanced down at Chloe and Captain. "And keep those disgusting animals away from me."

I handed Chloe's lead to Josie and followed Jessica and Jerry back inside the arena. I sat down in the seat Jerry pointed at and saw Josie in the doorway holding both leads and starting to slowly work her way toward me. Jessica and Jerry were chatting about how to handle the interview and didn't notice her stealthy approach.

"Okay, let's get going," Jessica said, transitioning back into her on-camera persona. "I'll keep my questions simple, you keep your answers short, and we'll both get out of this unscathed."

"Deal," I said.

I spent the next five minutes answering her questions that were focused on the dog show and our rescue program. The interview, as promised, was short and relatively painless, and when Alexandra nodded at Jerry that she was done, I caught Jackson's eye, and he wandered over. Josie saw him, and she took a few steps closer then stopped again. The dogs sat down on either side of her, and she held up her phone and looked through the viewfinder.

"Hey, Suzy," Jackson said. "Was you just on the TV?"

"Not yet, Jackson," I said, trying not to laugh at his bumpkin routine. "But I will be tonight. Right, Jessica?"

"What? Oh, yeah. It'll be on the eleven o'clock news," she said, tossing her microphone to Jerry and exhaling loudly.

"Wow. A real TV star in my midst," Jackson said. "You're Jessica Talbot, aren't you?"

"Yes, I am," Jessica said, flashing a quick smile. "Thanks for watching."

"You sure are purdy," Jackson said through the bulge in his cheek. "You wouldn't happen to be looking for a boyfriend now would you?"

Jessica gave him a blank stare.

"You're joking, right?" she said, dumbfounded.

"No, I ain't jokin'. I'm a lot of fun once you get to know me."

"And get past the smell?" she said. "Look, Bubba, I don't mean to be rude, but there are probably dogs here I'd date before I agreed to be seen anywhere in public with you. And just so we're perfectly clear, I hate dogs."

"That's okay. We don't have to go out. We could just go to my place," Jackson said, winking at her.

"Is that a wink, or an involuntary tic?" Jessica said. "If I were you, I'd get checked for Lyme disease."

Jackson nodded then added his own personal touch we hadn't discussed that surprised me. And shocked Jessica. Jackson worked up a healthy gob of tobacco juice and launched it at her foot. It landed in the perfect spot on her open-toed stiletto. I grimaced when I saw the sticky brown slime dripping down her pink pedicure.

"You're a lot nicer on TV, lady," Jackson said, giving me a quick wink as he wandered away.

"That's because they pay me to be nice on TV," she snapped, sitting down next to me and reaching into her purse for a tissue.

I nodded at Josie, and she removed Captain and Chloe's lead. She whispered something to them, and they dashed toward me, and I gently patted the edge of Jessica's seat when they got close. Chloe hopped up into Jessica's lap, and she screamed and flailed her arms wildly. But it was when Captain stood on his back legs and pinned her against the back of her seat with his front paws that she completely lost the plot.

"Stop! Get down! Get these disgusting creatures off me. They're making me sick to my stomach," she screamed as she pushed Chloe away, but found Captain a bit more of a handful to deal with.

Captain gently placed a front paw on Jessica's head which added bad hair day to her list of problems, and she screamed again and let loose with a litany of expletives that was both creative and extremely loud. Several people in the audience heard her outburst and were now paying close attention to the commotion. Jessica noticed and tried to calm herself.

"Get this animal off me," she whispered through clenched teeth.

"He's just really affectionate," I said, laughing. "Aren't you, Captain?"

Captain snorted, shook his head violently and a long strand of drool came loose from his jowls, floated through the air, then landed on Jessica's forehead and began sliding down toward her eyes. I tapped my seat and Captain released her and draped himself over me. I rubbed his head as his tail thumped loudly against Jessica's leg.

Jessica glanced up and blinked as the strand of drool dripped into her eyes and her blood-curdling howl echoed around the arena. She tried to scramble out of her seat but ended up tumbling backward and landing on the cement floor. She let loose with another string of expletives as she scrambled to her feet and jerked her skirt back down to a more ladylike length.

She sat back down in the row behind me breathing heavily. She pushed her hair back into place and glared at me as I continued to rub Captain's head.

"I hate everything about you and this place. Between the local hillbillies and filthy dogs, I don't know what's worse. Places like this should be blown off the face of the earth."

"Geez, Jessica," Josie deadpanned, still holding her phone. "I'm not sure comments like that or your overall attitude is going to play very well in Middle America."

Jessica flinched, then she looked at Jerry.

"Please tell me you didn't have the camera on during all of that."

"No, and I'll never forgive myself," Jerry said, unable to stop laughing.

"Don't worry, Jerry," Josie said. "I got all of it."

She waved her phone in the air.

"I want a copy," he said, wiping the tears out of his eyes.

"Just grab it off YouTube," Josie said. "I'll try to post it before I go to bed tonight."

"You set me up," Jessica said.

"Yeah, I guess we kinda did," I said, extricating myself from Captain and standing up. "How's it feel?"

"Okay, you made your point," she snapped. "Now what?"

"Well, I think these two hillbillies need to grab a glass of shine and discuss our next steps," I said, reattaching Chloe's lead. "We'll be in touch."

"The next time I see you, you're a dead woman," Jessica said, glaring at me.

"I'm still recording, Jessica," Josie said.

Jessica let loose with another string of expletives, then rubbed her forehead and got a handful of dog slobber. She looked around for somewhere to wipe her hand, then shook her head and slumped over in her seat. Josie and I headed for the foyer and handed Chloe and Captain's lead to Jill.

"Thanks for keeping an eye on these guys while we're inside. Is anything happening at the Inn?" I said.

"No, I just called, and it's pretty quiet. Which makes sense since it looks like the whole town is here," Jill said. "Rooster is teaching Sammy how to play cribbage."

"Just don't let Sammy play him for money," Josie said. "Rooster took a hundred bucks off me a couple months ago. And I know how to play."

"I'll give him the warning."

"That was fun," Josie said, as we strolled back inside the arena.

"A little nasty, don't you think?"

"She had it coming. Hey, since when does Jackson chew tobacco?"

"He doesn't. But that was a nice touch. Did we go too far?"

"Will you relax? It was just a bit of rather clever payback. And I doubt if Jessica is going to be much of a problem now."

"No, but maybe we should try to do something nice for her at some point if we get the chance," I said.

"Are you out of your mind?"

"Well, as my mother likes to say, it's always better to have somebody who owes you a favor, than it is to make them an enemy with revenge on their mind."

"Your mother said that?"

"She did once."

"When was that?"

"Right after she did something nice for me."

Chapter 15

I sat next to my mother during the show and divided my time between enjoying the dogs and scanning the crowd for the mysterious dognappers. My mother, not being much of a dog person, tolerated the parade of eleven different breeds and their handlers as they individually presented themselves to Alexandra then trotted down the carpet and back to often wild applause. But my mother was beaming, and I knew that the smile on her face was because the dog show was a huge success and a positive news story about our town, all too rare of late, would be shown on TV later this evening.

"I haven't seen anything worth noting yet," I whispered.

"How can someone who loves dogs as much as you do say that, darling?" my mother said, baffled. "I thought the ones from the breed you called the Clamper were delightful."

"It's the *Clumber*, Mom," I said, shaking my head.

But the four Clumbers had been fun to watch as Alexandra put them through their paces. A few years ago, we'd rescued one, and he was with us for a few months until he was adopted by an elderly couple who summered in the area. I still remembered the good times we'd had with the low-slung dog that loved to quietly hang out indoors but came to life whenever he hit the fresh air. Despite his wonderful personality and love of people, the dog had a stubborn streak that rivaled my Mom's, and he wasn't shy about displaying it when the mood struck.

"Clumber?" my mother said, frowning. "Are you sure, darling?"

"Pretty sure, Mom. And for the record, I was talking to Chief Abrams."

My mother glanced around the immediate area, then stared at me waiting for an explanation. I touched the earpiece I was wearing and casually pointed to the lavalier microphone attached to my collar. I glanced around the packed arena at the sea of faces and realized I was probably wasting my time.

"You need to seek professional help, darling."

"Sure, sure," I said, casually scanning the crowd. I lowered my head and whispered. "You see the guy in the bright blue sweater in the back row of section nine? He looks very suspicious."

"I'll remember to tell Detective Jones that when I see him," Chief Abrams said into my ear.

"Oh, he's a cop," I whispered. "Never mind."

"Josie told me what you two did to Jessica earlier," my mother said.

"Yeah, sorry about that, Mom. It's probably not one of my better moments."

"I wouldn't worry about it, darling. It was quite clever," she said, applauding politely as the long line of Labrador Retrievers entered the show area. "But what are you going to do now?"

"I'm going to do something nice for Jessica the first chance I get, Mom."

"Good girl," she said, patting my knee.

"Are you still mad at me for the way I behaved the other day?"

"No, I'm over it," she said, staring down at the dogs.

"And you've decided to just let it go?"

"Oh, no. Of course not, darling," she said, flashing me a quick smile. "But I'm no longer mad at you."

"You want me to do something nice for you, don't you?" I said.

"That would be wonderful."

"What is it?"

"I'll let you know, darling."

Josie, sitting on the other side of my mother, snorted.

"I'm going to have a chat with Chief Abrams."

I got up and headed down the walkway that led to the dog holding area.

"Did you see something?" Chief Abrams whispered into my ear.

"No, I'm just dealing with a flesh wound my Mom just gave me," I said. "Where are you?"

"Two sections over on your right. I'll meet you at the spot where they're holding all the Goldens."

Five minutes later, I was holding two cups of coffee and admiring the impressive collection of Golden Retrievers that were waiting for their turn. When Chief Abrams approached, I handed him one of the coffees.

"Thanks," he said. "No news from the Inn?"

"No, I just called again, and it's quiet over there," I said, frowning.

"You seem disappointed."

"I can't believe how stupid I am sometimes."

"Not a word I would use to describe you," he said, studying my face. "But go on. What's bothering you?"

"We were so concerned about the safety of Alexandra's dogs that we did everything possible to make sure nobody knew where they were," I said, shaking my head.

"And how could the dognappers steal them if they didn't where to look for them?"

"Exactly."

"That's actually a good point," he said. "We were so sure they'd stick out here at the show, I didn't even think about that."

"Me either. Probably not our best work, huh?"

"No, it's not. But let's not tell anybody," he said, laughing.

"And we completely underestimated the number of people from out of town who'd be here today," I said.

"Yup, we sure did," he said, sipping his coffee. "I don't recognize half the people here."

"We're going to need to catch a break," I said. "Nothing new from Rooster's cousin?"

"No, I think Coke Bottle told Rooster everything he knew yesterday."

"I'd love to figure out a way to set them up," I said. "I know they're dying to get their hands on those dogs."

"But we'd have to find a way to let the information about where the dogs are to casually slip out. It's not like we can just announce it over the PA system."

"You know, Chief. If the dognappers are some of the people who are showing dogs today, we could wander up and down the different holding areas chatting about Alexandra and her dogs, dropping clues along the way."

"Well, since I don't have any other ideas, I wouldn't feel good saying what a complete waste of time that would probably be."

"So, you think it's a dumb idea?" I said, raising an eyebrow at him.

"Yeah," he said. "But I don't feel good about telling you."

"Funny. Come on. All of a sudden, I'm feeling particularly chatty."

We spent the next fifteen minutes walking up and down the eleven holding areas engaged in casual conversation. When it became all too apparent that everyone we walked past was much more concerned about their dogs than anything the police chief and his babbling companion had to say, we gave up and leaned against a wall.

"Well, that's fifteen minutes of my life I'll never get back," I said, scuffing at the linoleum floor with one of my sneakers.

"Yeah, definitely not our best work," Chief Abrams said.

"Don't worry, I won't tell anybody," I said. "I wouldn't feel good about it."

Chapter 16

In the end, Margaret's Springer Spaniel not only won Best in Breed but also won Best in Group as the overall top dog. Glen and Abby Wilson's Chesapeake Bay Retriever finished second and judging from their frozen smiles as Alexandra presented them with their ribbon and prize money, they weren't very happy about again coming up a bit short. Rooster's ex-wife beamed and hugged her dog as she accepted the first prize trophy.

When Alexandra finished handing out all the awards, she handed the microphone to my mother who addressed the crowd, thanked everyone for coming, and announced that she hoped to see them all at next year's event. Then she launched into a preview of other events that would be held in town during the winter and spring.

"Well, I guess we know how we'll be spending Thanksgiving from now on," Josie said.

"A community Thanksgiving dinner followed by a dog show?" I said, shrugging. "I can think of a lot worse ways to spend it."

"Absolutely," Josie said, studying my mother as she continued addressing the crowd. "You know, for somebody who hates being mayor as much as she does, your Mom sure does a great job faking it."

"Yeah," I said, watching Jessica interviewing the winners. "Does that remind you of anybody?"

Josie focused on Jessica.

"Maybe a little," she said. "But your mom has a heart and fakes it for the right reasons. You think she expects us to say goodbye to Jessica and thank her?"

"What do you think?"

"Okay, but let's keep it short," Josie said, following me down to the floor of the arena.

We waited for Jessica to finish her interview with my mother. When they finished, my mother caught my eye and gave me her best *play nice* look then started chatting with Alexandra. Jessica tossed her microphone to Jerry and exhaled loudly. She looked worn out, and I decided that she had probably been working pretty much non-stop since she'd arrived three days ago. When she saw us, her face fell flat.

"Let me guess," Jessica said. "You want to give me a guided tour of your still."

"Funny. No, we just stopped by to thank you for everything you've done," I said.

"Don't mention it," she said. "That's what they pay me to do."

"Well, thanks anyway," I said. "Maybe our paths will cross again."

"I seriously doubt that," she said, giving me a blank stare. "This time next year, I'll be Christmas shopping in Manhattan while the two of you will be stuck here in this-"

"Charming little hamlet?" Josie said.

"Sure," Jessica said, giving Josie an evil grin. "Let's go with that."

"I take it that today didn't do anything to change your mind about dogs?" Josie said.

"Are you kidding? The only thing today did was give me two hundred more reasons to hate the filthy creatures."

"How is that possible?" Josie said.

"Actually, it's quite easy," she said, flipping her hair back with a shake of her head. "And if that video shows up anywhere, my lawyer will be in touch."

"Don't worry, Jessica," I said. "*Both* videos will be safe and sound with us."

"Hey, not so fast," Josie said. "I was planning to use the shot of her going over the back of her chair for next year's Christmas card. I'm still working on the caption."

"Let it go, Josie," I said, then looked at Jessica. "If you drop the idea of using the footage of me in the hunting camp, we won't do anything with the one we got today."

Jessica considered my proposal for several seconds, then nodded.

"Deal. The video of you holding the knife doesn't help with my new image we're working on anyway," she said. "But I don't want to have to worry about the one of me showing up online at some point in the future. I'm going to have to insist that you agree to delete both of them."

"Delete is such a strong word," Josie said.

I punched Josie on the arm.

"Ow. Okay, as soon as Chief Abrams and your lawyers give us the word, we'll delete both of them," Josie said.

"I want to be here when you do it," Jessica said.

"I'll give you a call," I said. "I guess our paths will be crossing again, huh?"

"Only a brief intersection," she said, nodding at Jerry that she was ready to go. "Okay, if you'll excuse me, ladies. I'm going to head home to take a long shower followed by a hot bath and, if necessary, a disinfectant rubdown. After that, I'm going to get drunk."

She strode off, stepping around a collection of people and dogs that were mingling near the exit. Jerry the Cameraman watched her leave and shook his head.

"She's a piece of work," Jerry said.

"Not one of her better days, huh?" I said.

"Actually, this was one of her good ones," he said. "Everybody at the station can't wait for her to go to New York."

"You think she's going to get that new show?" I said.

"Just as long as she keeps Bob happy," he said, tossing his bag over a shoulder.

"How could that woman possibly make anybody happy?" Josie said.

"Use your imagination."

"Yeah. Never mind. Dumb question," Josie said. "And after that?"

"Oh, she'll drop Bob like he was yesterday's news. I'm sure Jessica already has her sights on the next guy who'll be able to help her climb the next couple of rungs after she lands in New York."

"What a way to go through life," I said.

"Yeah, I used to think that," Jerry said. "And don't get me wrong, she works really hard. But Jessica's devotion to her own self-interests combined with her complete indifference to other people is probably what's driving all her success."

"Indifference like she gets from her cat?" Josie said.

"Cat? Jessica doesn't have a cat," Jerry said, laughing. "She has a pet snake. A ten-foot python she keeps in her living room. The only time you'd see a cat in her house would be if she was feeding it to the snake."

"That's disgusting," I said.

"She keeps the snake as a reminder," Jerry said. "It's a metaphor for her approach to life. Stalk, devour, digest, then move on."

"You're joking, right?" Josie said.

"I wish," he said, adjusting the bag on his shoulder. "Jessica's been known to trash the reputation of a lot of people she worked with after she's *moved on.*"

"And that's why you want a copy of today's tape?" Josie said.

"That's part of it," he said. "Mainly I'd like to have it because it's one of the funniest things I've ever seen."

"I'll see what I can do," Josie said.

"Yeah," he said, studying Josie's expression. "From what I've seen, I believe you will."

"Take care, Jerry," I said. "Thanks for all your help."

"Suzy, Josie, it's been so nice meeting you," he said, bowing slightly. "Today was great. You know, I've been thinking about adopting a dog, and now I know just the place to find one when I'm ready."

"Just let us know," Josie said. "What kind of dog are you looking for?"

"Well, I've been thinking about getting a Rottweiler, but now that it looks like Jessica is leaving, I'll probably go with something a bit smaller. Those Springer Spaniels looked pretty good."

"Good choice," Josie said.

"Don't forget about sending me a copy of that video," he said, handing Josie one of his cards.

"You mean the video that was shot by some unknown person in the audience?" Josie said, raising an eyebrow.

"That's exactly the one I'm talking about," he said, waving goodbye.

We watched him make his way toward to the exit, then I turned to Josie.

"You wouldn't," I said.

"He probably just wants it as a keepsake," Josie said.

"A keepsake?"

"Yeah. A reminder of a special event in one's life."

"I know what it means, Josie. But if we agree to delete it, and then it shows up later on, won't Jessica and her lawyers know where it came from?"

"Suzy, there were several hundred people here today carrying Smartphones. Good luck proving it came from me."

I thought about it, then nodded.

"You got a good point there," I said. "Remind me never to get on your bad side."

"By now, I'm surprised you need a reminder," she said, punching me hard on the shoulder.

"Ow!"

"You thought I forgot, huh?"

Chapter 17

The arena had pretty much emptied out by the time we retrieved Captain and Chloe. I hugged my mom on her way out, helped our crew pack up, then we chatted with Jill and were happy to hear that five dogs had been adopted during the day. Then Josie and I headed back inside the arena and made our way to the converted supply closet where Alexandra was finishing up the last of her paperwork. Chloe sat down next to me as I worked my way into the cramped space and stood next to the small desk. Captain and Josie were relegated to the doorway since there was no absolutely no room for them.

"I'm almost done," Alexandra said, scribbling notes furiously on a series of forms.

"Long day for you," I said.

"Yes, for a show this size there would normally be at least three judges, but I managed to get through it. And it was a very good show," she said, tapping the forms into a neat stack and sliding them into her bag. "Did you have any luck finding the people who are trying to steal Lucky and Lucy?"

"No, we completely whiffed on that."

"And nothing has happened at the Inn?"

"Absolutely not. And we called every half-hour to get an update," I said. "Your dogs are fine. And Josie and I would like to invite you to stay with us until you leave for home."

"Out of concern that those people will try again?" Alexandra said.

"That's part of it," I said, shrugging. "But we thought you might be more comfortable there than in a motel."

"I'm quite used to motels," she said, smiling. "I really don't want to put you out. I'm sure we'll be fine."

"At least stay for dinner when you stop by to pick them up," Josie said.

"That I can do," Alexandra said.

Chloe emitted a soft guttural growl that lasted several seconds.

"What's the matter, girl?" I said, rubbing her head. "I know we're a bit late with your dinner, but there's no need to grumble."

Chloe continued her low growl. I glanced around the closet and looked at Josie. She didn't see me because she was looking down at Captain who was also beginning to growl.

"What the heck is up with these two?" I said.

"No idea."

Then Chloe starting barking and stood on her back legs with her front paws planted on the desk. She was staring up at the open ceiling, and her barks turned into a snarl. I glanced up, caught a glimpse of a hand, then saw one of the boxes on the catwalk above begin to drop. I jerked Chloe back by the collar with one hand and used the other to pull Alexandra out of her chair. She stumbled forward a few steps before Josie caught her, and the box from above loudly crashed on top of the chair where Alexandra had just been sitting.

"Okay, this is not good," I said, as I heard the sound of footsteps on the catwalk. "We need to get into the hallway where at least we'll have a roof over our heads."

"You and Chloe just saved my life," Alexandra whispered, staring at the box.

We got Captain and Chloe settled down a bit, and I kept listening to the sound of fading footsteps.

"What do you want to do?" Josie said.

"I'm not sure," I said, glancing up and down the hallway. "Chief Abrams has already gone home."

"Do I need to remind you that getting the heck out of here would be an outstanding choice?" Josie whispered.

"Hang on. Just give me a second to think."

Then the lights went out.

In the total darkness, the only sound I could hear now was the low, steady growl coming from both dogs.

"What is it with these people and light switches?" Josie said.

"Shhh."

Moments later, the emergency lights came on and an eerie dim wash of light filled the arena. I heard the sound of movement coming from inside the large storage area where the Zamboni was kept.

147

"Alexandra, I need you to do us a favor?" I said.

"You do?"

"Yes. Could you take Chloe and Captain out the emergency exit you'll see about fifty feet down the hall? It'll take you right outside."

"Good plan," Josie said. "I strongly suggest we tag along."

"Hang on," I said, placing a hand on Josie's forearm. "Here's my phone, Alexandra. Call Chief Abrams and explain what happened. When he gets here, just get in the police car with the dogs and wait for us."

"What are you going to do?" Alexandra said.

"I have an idea," I said.

"Geez, I really hate it when that happens," Josie said.

"Please don't do anything crazy," Alexandra said.

"Listen to her, Suzy," Josie said.

"Shhh," I said, placing a finger to my lips. "Go ahead, Alexandra. As long as those people are inside the arena, you and the dogs will be safe."

Alexandra nodded, and we gave the dogs a quick pet then handed their leads to her. She started to walk away, then stopped and turned back.

"You know, maybe I will accept your generous offer to stay with you," she said.

"Good call," Josie said.

Alexandra briskly walked off with the dogs, and we waited until we heard the emergency exit door open and shut. Then I looked at Josie.

"Okay, just follow my lead," I said.

"You mean like doing something really stupid?"

"Funny. Just keep your voice down."

I slowly started working my way down the hallway. Josie followed close behind. Then she stepped on the back of my sneaker, and it came off.

"Sorry about that," she whispered. "Maybe we should take that as a harbinger."

"A harbinger?" I said, kneeling down to put my shoe back on.

"Yeah, an omen of something very bad that's about to happen."

"Shut it," I said, resuming my slow walk down the hallway.

When we reached the door to the storage area, I stopped and slowly tested the handle. It was locked.

"You know what this means, don't you?" I said.

"That we can go home?"

"No, it means there's a good chance they might be trapped in there."

"That's good," she whispered. "All we need to do is wait for the Chief."

"We need to do one thing before he gets here," I said.

"Disagree."

"Stay here. I'll be right back."

"Where on earth are you going?"

"Shhh."

I trotted down the hallway to the converted closet then grabbed the letter opener I'd noticed earlier on the desk. I headed back and ignored the angry glare Josie was giving me.

"This door has one of those cheap button locks. All I need to do is work this into the keyhole, and it should pop right open."

"You are so gonna pay for this, Suzy."

"I'm well aware of that. Now, keep your voice down and try to follow my lead when we get in there."

I jammed the letter envelope in and fiddled with it for a few seconds before I heard a soft click. I turned the handle and pushed the door open partway. I looked over my shoulder and nodded for Josie to follow me. I crouched as I stepped inside then worked my way to the right. Through the dim light, I could see stacks of boxes and bags containing supplies. The Zamboni sat in the center of the room, and the hockey boards were stacked along one side of the large space.

"Lots of places to hide," I whispered.

"I'm glad to hear that. Pick a good one," she whispered.

"Relax. They're not after us."

"Not yet."

Near one of the stacks, I heard what sounded like cardboard being slid across concrete. It didn't last long, but it was clear that one of the boxes had moved.

"Okay, they're definitely in here," I whispered. "Here we go."

I took a few steps forward, cleared my throat, and spoke in a loud, clear voice.

"See, there's nobody here. I told you that box just happened to fall off the catwalk."

I waited for Josie's response but got nothing out of her. I punched her on the shoulder.

"Ow," she whispered. "What was that for?"

"That was your cue," I whispered.

"Oh. Okay, I got it," she whispered, then said in a big voice. "Sorry about that. You know me, always looking for conspiracies."

"You watch too many cop shows. Nobody is after Alexandra. All they want to do is steal her dogs."

"You think the dogs will be safe while they're staying with us?" Josie said, glancing around the storage area.

"They'll be fine, but I am a little worried about Tuesday night. We'll all be at that thing."

"What thing?" Josie whispered.

"How would I know?" I whispered back. "A thing. Just make something up."

"Oh, that's right," she called out. "I completely forgot. That's the night of the awards banquet. And they want all of us to be there, right?"

"Since we're getting an award for the Inn, we can't really leave any of the staff behind, right?"

"No, that wouldn't be fair."

"I just wish the guy who's coming to fix our security system could get here before Wednesday," I said.

"There's no way he can move it up?"

"No, he's booked solid. We'll be able to keep a close eye on things the rest of the time, but Tuesday night the place will be unguarded. But all the dogs should be okay, don't you think?"

"Yeah, we've never had a problem before," Josie said. "I'm sure we'll be just fine."

"I'd ask Chief Abrams to keep an eye on the place, but he starts vacation on Tuesday."

"Oh, that's right. Where's he going again?"

I glared at Josie.

"Who cares where he's going?" I whispered.

"Well, excuse me for trying to add a little color to the story," she whispered back.

"I think he's going to Hawaii," I said, refocusing. "Jimmy will be in charge while he's gone, but he always refuses to leave the office."

"Yeah, I heard he just sits at his desk and plays solitaire on his computer," Josie said, then glanced at me.

Although I didn't have a clue who Jimmy was, the cover story sounded plausible, so I shrugged and continued.

"Can we go home now?" I said.

"Yeah, sorry about freaking out like that. That box really scared me when it fell."

"Don't worry about it," I said. "But the maintenance staff needs to do a better job of storing stuff up there."

I nodded at the door, and we stepped outside, closing the door behind us.

"Okay, I think that's about all we can do for now," I said.

"Then let's go," Josie said. "I'm starving."

The lights in the arena returned to full power, and moments later we saw Chief Abrams walking down the hallway toward us. His gun was in his right hand by his side.

"Are you guys, okay?" he said, glancing around.

"Yeah, we're fine," I said. "What about Alexandra and the dogs?"

"They're on their way home. I called Jackson, and he picked them up a couple of minutes ago," he said, sliding his gun back into its holster. "You want to catch me up?"

We did, and he listened closely. When we finished, he glanced at the door to the storage area.

"They're still in there?" he said.

"I think so," I said. "They sure didn't come through that door."

"The parking lot is empty."

"Then they must be on foot," I said.

"Well, let me go have a look," he said, removing his gun again.

"Why don't we just wait for them to show up Tuesday night?" I said.

"Because they're suspects in the murder of Rooster's brother. And I can arrest them right now for unlawful entry and, if I get real lucky, attempted murder," he snapped. "Are those good enough reasons for you?"

"There's no need to get snarky, Chief," I said.

"Just stay put here and out of the way," he said, one-part cop, one-part father.

He slowly opened the door and stepped inside the now brightly lit area. I leaned against the wall and tapped a foot.

"I don't see why we couldn't just wait until Tuesday night and catch them red-handed," I said, pouting.

"Unbelievable," Josie said, shaking her head.

A few minutes later, Chief emerged from the storage area. He holstered his gun and took another look up and down the hallway.

"They're gone," he said.

"How the heck did they get out?" I said.

"Well, if my cop intuition is right, my guess is that they went out the door on the other side of the storage area."

"Oh. I didn't notice another door," I said. "But in our defense, it was pretty dark in there."

"You can leave me out of this one, Sherlock," Josie said.

"Then we're back to our Tuesday night plan," I said, smiling. "Oh, before I forget, Chief, you might want to keep a low profile during the day on Tuesday."

"And why would I do that?"

"Because you're supposed to be heading for Hawaii," Josie said.

"I am?"

"Yeah," I said. "It just came up when we were creating the cover story."

"Hawaii. Nice. Which island?"

"Does it matter?" I said, frowning.

"Probably only if I was actually going," he deadpanned. "But I've always wanted to pretend I was going to Maui."

Chapter 18

When we got home, we found Chef Claire and a still rattled Alexandra in the living room with the dogs. The four Goldens along with Captain and Chloe were all stretched out in front of the roaring fire but stirred when we entered. Except for Chloe, the dogs soon resumed their positions and nodded off. Chloe hopped up onto the couch and dropped her head in my lap.

"There's my little hero," I said, stroking her fur. "How are you doing, Alexandra?"

"I've been better," she said. "But the wine seems to be helping."

"Not to be too blunt, Alexandra," I said. "But do you have any idea of who might want to kill you?"

"No," she whispered. "Stealing my dogs is one thing, but trying to kill me is something else altogether."

"Yes, it is. But can you think of anybody from the show today that could have been involved? You mentioned before that some people were jealous of your success," I said.

Alexandra thought about my question for several moments before shaking her head.

"Petty jealousies are common. But murder is something else altogether," she said.

"Maybe they were hired by someone else to get the dogs and kill Alexandra," Josie said.

Alexandra flinched when she heard Josie's comment. I considered Josie's idea then frowned.

"No, I don't think so," I said, thinking out loud. "If they were contract killers, the results would be a lot better than what we've seen so far."

"Better?" Alexandra said, staring at me.

"I'm sorry, Alexandra," I said. "I didn't mean it that way. If they were professionals, I doubt they would have gone about their business in such a slipshod way. Up to this point, we have somebody getting stabbed with a kitchen knife, and you almost getting conked on the head with a box. Instead of pros, I think we're dealing with a couple of highly motivated amateurs."

"That really doesn't make me feel a lot better," Alexandra said.

"I'm sure it doesn't," I said. "But it does increase the chances that they'll make another mistake. Like the one they're about to make on Tuesday night."

Josie and I provided an update on what had happened since Alexandra left the arena with the dogs.

"Do you really think they'll show up Tuesday night?" Alexandra said.

"I do. They're motivated, and we just gave them the opportunity they think they'll need."

"To steal the dogs, yes," Alexandra said. "But that doesn't deal with my other problem. The one where someone wants to kill me."

"But if we catch them in the act trying to steal the dogs, then we'll be able to remove that threat as well," I said. "I really think we've got a great chance to wrap this up Tuesday night."

"You're convinced that the people who want to steal the dogs are the same people who are trying to kill me?"

"I'd be shocked if it wasn't, Alexandra."

"Yes. I'm sure you're right. I need to call Harold to see if he can cut his business trip short," she said, getting up out of her chair.

Alexandra headed for the guest bedroom to make the call and Josie stretched out in front of the fire next to the dogs. Captain raised his head briefly, then draped one of his front paws over her shoulder and went back to sleep.

"You're thinking about organizing a greeting party for our visitors on Tuesday night, aren't you?" Josie said.

"Yeah. I thought we'd start with Chief Abrams and Rooster. Maybe Chief will ask the state police to send somebody as well."

"So, I get to spend Tuesday night in the condo area sitting in the dark waiting for a couple of dognappers to show up?" Josie said.

"I suppose it would be okay for you to stay in the reception area."

"Not a chance," she said, yawning. "If I'm going to be down there all night, I'm spending it with the dogs."

"Bring along a couple bags of the bite-sized Snickers to keep you company," I said.

"You can bet on that," she said, closing her eyes.

"Before you ask," Chef Claire said. "I'll be working. And Al and Dente will be in the lounge with Rocco keeping a very close eye on them."

"I wasn't going to ask you," I said.

"Good. I hate disappointing you," she said, laughing. "I don't want to get anywhere near them. That is unless you catch them. And if you do, my softball bat and I would love to have a little chat with them."

Alexandra walked back into the living room wiping tears from her eyes. She slumped down into a chair and dropped her head, her shoulders shaking.

"What happened?" I said.

"My husband said it's too late for him to change his plans," she said, continuing to sob. "In fact, he said his trip needs to be extended."

Josie sat up and looked at me. The idea that a husband wouldn't drop everything he was doing to get home after his wife had gone through what Alexandra had seemed callous.

"He's such a workaholic," Alexandra said. "And this just confirms what I've always known. Everybody plays second fiddle to money. I'm sorry you have to sit here and watch me blubber like a baby."

"Don't worry about that," I said. "What's the business deal he's working on that's so important?"

"He's been trying to close a big endorsement deal with a company that sells a variety of dog products. We thought we had it wrapped up a few weeks ago, but the company is having second thoughts about using Lucky and Lucy. Apparently, their internal market research indicates that the popularity of Golden Retrievers has peaked, and they've started looking at using a different breed."

"What's the company's name?" Josie said.

"Fetch and Tug."

"Good company," Josie said. "We sell some of their products. What breed is the company thinking about using?"

"Chesapeake Bay Retrievers," Alexandra said.

"Like the one that Glen and Abby Wilson have?" I said, the hairs on the back of my neck starting to tingle.

"Not like it," Alexandra whispered. "They're thinking about using their dog."

"Well, maybe the dog's second place finish today will help change Fetch and Tug's mind," Josie said, glancing over at me.

"That would be wonderful," Alexandra said through a half-grimace, half-smile. "But I'm afraid the process has gone too far for that to make any real difference."

"Did your husband have any suggestions about what you should do?" I said, still having a hard time believing that the man wasn't already on an airplane heading this way.

"I explained that I'd be staying here for a few days. And I told him that you were quite confident that we would be able to put an end to this on Tuesday night. As soon as he heard that, he relaxed and told me he was going to stay put. So, I told him not to worry and that I was in good hands. But he suggested that I head to my sister's on Wednesday instead of going home. Then we made plans to connect next week in Massachusetts. I'm judging another Sporting Group show outside of Boston next Saturday."

"Where does your sister live?" I said.

"She has a horse farm outside of Saratoga Springs."

"Just to be safe," I said. "If we don't get them Tuesday night, I think you should probably hire some security to keep an eye on you and your dogs until you can reconnect with your husband."

"That's probably a good idea," Alexandra said, pushing herself up out of the chair. "I hate to do this, but I'm exhausted, and I think I'll turn in."

"Don't you want to have dinner first?" Chef Claire said.

"Perhaps I'll have a bite to eat later if I wake up. But it's been a very long and trying day."

"We understand," I said. "Sleep well."

She smiled at us, whistled softly, and Lucky and Lucy woke up and followed her as she left the room.

161

"What sort of husband doesn't come running when his wife goes through something like that?" Josie said.

"One who is very focused on making money," I said.

"I remember her making a comment about their relationship before," Chef Claire said. "It sounded like she was describing a business partnership rather than a marriage."

"Well, they have two adult kids," I said. "So they've obviously been married a long time. The relationship has probably changed over the years."

"Yeah, I get that," Josie said. "But still. I think not coming home is a crappy thing for him to do."

"The Fetch and Tug deal must be worth a lot of money," I said.

"And you're thinking that the Abby and Glen Wilson might be doing everything they can to make sure nothing happens that could screw it up?" Josie said.

"I'm trying not to think that," I said.

"But you're failing miserably, right?" Chef Claire said.

"I certainly am."

Chapter 19

Temperatures in the low thirties combined with cold rain and a brisk north wind always limits the number of activities one might agree to participate in on a day like this. But this type of weather, that kept most people tight-lipped and hunkered down whenever they stepped outside seemed appropriate for a trip to a funeral home.

Josie and I, wearing hooded rain slickers, pushed forward across the parking lot holding our struggling umbrellas at a thirty-degree angle in front of us to fend off the wind and rain.

"When do we leave for Grand Cayman?" Josie yelled above the howling wind.

"Not soon enough."

We finally reached the covered entrance to the funeral home and shook the excess water off our umbrellas and slid them into a stand outside the door. Moments later, my mother parked under the covered area and hopped out of her car. An attendant handed her a ticket, and she handed over a five to the young man. He hopped in the car and drove off. My mother smiled, then frowned at the confused look on our faces.

"Hello, ladies," she said. "You two look like a couple of drowned rats. For the record, it's not your best look."

"Since when does Godfrey offer valet parking, Mom?"

"Ever since it started raining, darling," she said, the smile returning.

"Funny. I guess I never noticed before," I said.

"Have you ever been here before on a rainy day?"

"That must be it, Mom. How are you doing?"

"I'm wonderful, darling. Still basking in the glow of the success of our recent events and the associated publicity."

"So the council and business owners are happy?" I said.

"They are delighted," she said, then changed gears. "Okay, Suzy. I know how you can get when you see things like this. Try to control yourself, please."

"What are you talking about?"

"Your rather delicate sensibilities," my mother said.

"Delicate sensibilities? I'm going to need a little clarification, Mom."

"Try not to throw up in the casket."

Josie snorted and waved to Godfrey Anderson, the owner of the funeral home, as she stepped inside. We followed her, and I removed my rain slicker and handed it to Godfrey. He'd bought the mortuary from his father a few years earlier and was a nice man who performed what I considered one of the worst jobs on the planet with a quiet, dignified professionalism that had earned him the respect of virtually everyone in town. But he constantly reeked of cologne that reminded me of a pine-scented disinfectant. I'd always assumed he was trying to overcompensate for spending so much time working with formaldehyde and other tools of the trade, but maybe he just liked the smell of pine.

I got a whiff of the cologne, spent a few seconds pondering the embalming process, and felt my stomach churn.

We briefly chatted with Godfrey, then entered the main viewing area where an open casket at the other end of the room was surrounded by various floral arrangements. I glanced around and couldn't help but notice attendance was light. I spotted Rooster sitting quietly by himself in the front row and approached.

"Hi, Rooster," I said, giving him a hug. "I'm so sorry about your brother."

"Thanks, Suzy. I appreciate that."

"You're wearing a suit for a second time this week. That must be some sort of record."

"Tell me about it," he said, chuckling. "You know, I've spent the last fifteen minutes sitting here trying to feel worse than I do. Shouldn't I be grieving?"

"I'm sure you are in your own way, Rooster, I said, sneaking a quick peek at the casket.

"I don't know if I've ever known a bigger screw up who completely wasted their life," he said, then sighed loudly.

I snuck another quick look at the casket, then felt my breakfast start working its way up my throat. I pressed my stomach with the palm of my hand and focused on my breathing.

"Is that your cousin?" I said, surprised to see him here.

"Yeah, he was released this morning," Rooster said. "The state police aren't looking at him for the murder, and I decided not to press charges for criminal trespassing and B&E."

"That was a very kind thing to do," I said.

"After what happened to my brother, I just couldn't go through with having him locked up," Rooster said. "I think I'm getting soft in my old age."

"I always knew you were a big puppy. So, what's he going to do now?"

"He is going to do exactly what I told him to do," Rooster said, glancing over at Coke Bottle who was sitting by himself in a long row of chairs that stretched along one wall. "I gave him another stack of cash, the last one he will ever get from me by the way, and told him that he needed to leave Clay Bay and never come back."

"I wish I could say I was going to miss him," I said. "But since he's stolen dogs from us twice now, I'd be lying."

"Yeah, I get that. Mean and stupid is not much of a way to go through life, huh?"

"Where do you think he'll land?"

"He's been talking about Florida," Rooster said. "And that's far enough away for me."

I watched Coke Bottle as he removed his glasses to dry his eyes. Then he stared off into the distance in his own little world as he wiped the thick lenses with a cleaning cloth. Godfrey strode past him and Coke Bottle, startled, jerked violently in his chair.

Then he pressed a hand against his chest and took several deep breaths to recover before putting his glasses back on.

"What an idiot," Rooster said.

"And obviously scared of his own shadow."

I snuck another peek at the casket. Repetition wasn't improving my reaction. I turned and saw my mother approaching just as a thought popped into my head. I glanced down at the thick carpet, then whispered into Rooster's ear. He listened carefully, then his eyes grew wide as he stared back at me. He nodded and was about to respond when my mother arrived.

"Well, look at the two of you," she said. "Whispering like a couple of thieves."

"Hey, Mom. I was just asking Rooster if he wanted to join us for a drink at C's after the viewing hours are over."

"That sounds like a great idea," he said. "I'm going to need one."

"I wish I could join you, but I have a meeting to go to," my mother said. "Rooster, again I am so sorry for your loss."

"Thanks, Mrs. C. I appreciate you stopping by."

"Hang in there, Rooster," she said, patting his arm. "Darling, I need to run."

"Me too, Mom," I said. "I'll walk out with you. I'll see you in a bit, Rooster. And since he's leaving town, bring your cousin along for a goodbye drink."

"I'll do that," he said.

I walked next to my mother back toward the front door where Josie was already waiting. She was holding her rain slicker in her hand.

"I have the thing you call a car being brought to the front," Josie said.

"Good thinking," I said, grabbing my slicker off the coatrack. "And it's an SUV."

"It's a noisy, leaky contraption that needs to be put out of its misery," my mother said. "Please, darling, let me take you car shopping."

"As soon as we get back from vacation, Mom. I promise."

We walked outside and stood under the covered area as the rain and wind continued unabated. My SUV was the first vehicle to arrive, and the valet hopped out and gave me an odd look.

"What?" I said, handing him a five.

"You'll see," he said, heading off to retrieve my mother's car.

Josie opened the passenger door, and a small flood poured out, soaking her feet. She glared at me.

"If you don't mind, I think I'll catch a ride with your mom."

"Sorry about that," I said, taking a quick look inside the SUV to see where the leaks were coming from. "I'll see you at the restaurant. Later, Mom."

I gave them a quick wave and hopped in the driver seat. I made the drive to C's dodging the rain streaming through a popped windshield seam while trying to keep my feet dry as water kicked up by my tires splashed through the hole in the floorboards.

The drive was short but extremely unpleasant.

Chapter 20

I entered the restaurant through the back door that led directly into the kitchen and found Chef Claire regaling two of her staff with a story about her days running a food truck on the West Coast. As opposed to the summer when the kitchen was hectic and loud, things were moving at a much slower and quieter pace that would continue most nights until spring arrived.

"Hey, Suzy," Chef Claire said, staring at me. "Let me guess. You and Chloe decided to roll around in the rain."

"My SUV sprung a couple of new leaks," I said.

"How could you tell?"

"Funny. Any chance you've got a change of clothes here?"

"Sorry. I just took everything I had here home to wash. The best I can do is one of the waitress uniforms."

"Checkerboard pants and a black blouse?" I said, frowning. "I guess I can make that work."

"They're hanging in the closet next to the shower," Chef Claire said.

"Thanks," I said, removing my soaked sneakers and socks. "Any chance I could use one of your ovens to dry these out?"

Chef Claire stared at me in disbelief.

"Yeah, that's what I thought," I said. "Never mind."

"I've got a pair of sandals somewhere you can wear."

"Perfect," I said, heading off.

"Oh, Suzy," Chef Claire said. "As soon as you get changed, I think table seven is ready to order."

"You're really not funny."

"To quote our good friend, disagree."

I made a face at her before heading off to change and another on my way out. I headed to the lounge and found it empty except for Rocco who was sitting in a chair in front of the fire laughing at Al and Dente. At the moment, they each had one end of a rubber chew toy in their mouths and were holding on for dear life in a game of tug of war.

Rocco did a double take when he saw what I was wearing.

"If you're thinking about moonlighting to pick up some extra cash, I suggest you come back in the summer when things pick up a bit."

"Everybody is a comedian," I said, kneeling down to pet the dogs.

They tolerated me interrupting their game for a few seconds, then resumed their attempts to acquire sole position of the toy.

"Can I get you anything?"

"Coffee with a shot of brandy sounds pretty good," I said, glancing around the empty lounge.

Rocco hopped up out of his chair and went to the bar. He returned shortly holding two large mugs.

"I think that's the one with the brandy," he said, handing me one of the mugs. "You just come from the memorial service?"

"Yeah. Not one of my favorite things to do," I said, taking a sip.

"Imagine how the guy in the box feels."

Josie came in the front door dripping water all over the mat in the foyer. She shook her umbrella then closed it and removed her rain slicker. She headed straight for the dogs and got the same reaction I did.

"You know what I like best about days like this?" she said, hugging Al.

"Nothing?"

"Exactly. Well, you were right. Your mother has invited six guys to dinner at her place in Grand Cayman the day we arrive."

"I knew it," I said. "Did she say who they were?"

"The usual suspects. A couple of lawyers, a banker, and some guys from one of the embassies down there," she said, looking up from the dogs and getting her first look at my waitress outfit. "Can I get a cup of coffee, please, Rocco?"

"No comments about what I'm wearing?"

"No, I'm speechless," Josie said. "But I probably would have gone with the chef uniform. You get to wear that cool hat."

The front door opened again, and Rooster and Coke Bottle stepped inside. They hung their coats up and entered the lounge. Coke Bottle stood near the entrance to the lounge, squinting as his eyes adjusted to the light, then sat down next to Rooster at the bar.

"Hi, Rooster," Rocco said. "What can I get you guys?"

"Two double shots of Remy Martin, thanks."

"You got it," Rocco said, pouring the drinks.

"Ain't you gonna ask me what I want?" Coke Bottle snapped.

Rooster sighed loudly and slid one of the drinks over to Coke Bottle.

"Oh, sorry," he mumbled. "I didn't know one of them was for me."

"Rocco," Rooster said. "I'd like you to meet my idiot cousin, Walter."

"Nice to meet you, Walter."

"Yeah, right back at ya'," Coke Bottle said, glaring at Rooster. "And I'm not an idiot. I'm just a little slow on the intake."

"Uptake," Rooster whispered, then downed his drink.

"What?"

"Nothing."

Josie and I pulled two barstools next to them, and the four of us sat in a small circle at the bar. We both ordered red wine when Rooster ordered two more doubles of Remy.

"Aren't you going to give me a menu?" Coke Bottle said, squinting at me.

"Actually, I don't work here. Don't you remember me?"

"Yeah, I recognize you two. You're the dog ladies," Coke Bottle said, squinting. "Sorry I took your dogs."

"Again," Josie said.

"Yeah. But you got 'em back both times. Rooster, I'm hungry."

"Memorial services always make you hungry, too?" Josie said.

"What?" Coke Bottle said, squinting in Josie's general direction.

"Don't worry about a menu," Rooster said. "We'll grab a bite later."

"Walter, your glasses fascinate me," I said. "Would you mind if I had a look at them?"

"What for?"

"I'd just like to see what it's like to look through them," I said, casually. "The lenses are so thick."

"I think I need a new pair," Coke Bottle said. "I'm having problems seeing things off in the distance."

"Call NASA," Josie said.

"What?" he said, frowning as he handed me his glasses.

"Wow," I said, holding them in my palm. "They're really heavy."

"Tell me about it. You should try wearing them around all day."

"They need to be cleaned," I said, hopping down off the barstool.

"Hang on," Coke Bottle said, reaching into his pocket. "I've got a cloth right here."

"That's okay," I said, heading for the bar and grabbing a cloth napkin.

Coke Bottle glanced around completely disoriented. He started waving his hands in an attempt to get his bearings. Josie leaned back in her barstool as his hands drifted close to her face. I slowly approached and stood next to him.

"Here you go, Walter," I said, loudly.

Startled, he swung around on his barstool and flailed his arms in the air. One of them landed, and I fell and somersaulted across the floor. I managed to get to my knees and grimaced as I tried to catch my breath.

"I'm sorry," Coke Bottle said, still waving his arms around. "I didn't see you there."

"Are you okay?" Rocco said, helping me to my feet.

"I'm fine," I said, checking my ribs for damage, "You pack quite a wallop, Walter. I'm just glad you weren't holding a knife."

Coke Bottle stopped flailing and sat quietly as tears began to form in his eyes. I placed the glasses in his hand, and he slowly put them back on. He looked at Rooster, tears now streaming down his face. I heard the sound of the front door slowly opening, and Chief Abrams appeared at the entrance to the lounge.

"I got your message," he said, glancing around and nodding hello to Rocco and Josie.

I held up a hand indicating that I wanted him to stay where he was for the moment. Coke Bottle's shoulders began to quake, and despite my contempt for him and the things he did, I felt a tinge of sympathy as I watched him deflate.

"Is there anything you want to tell me, Walter?" Rooster said, softly.

"It was an accident, Rooster," he whispered. "I'm so sorry. But you gotta believe me, it was an accident. I'd never do anything to hurt Jerry."

"I know you wouldn't, Walter," Rooster said. "You panicked when the lights went out, and your glasses fell off, didn't you?"

"Yeah."

"And the knife?" Rooster said, sounding as if he were trying to comfort a distraught child.

"I was using it to eat an apple," he said, then wailed loudly. "You don't need a knife to eat an apple. Why did I do something stupid like that, Rooster?"

"Walter, it's just what you do."

"What are you gonna do, Rooster?"

"That's a very good question." Rooster glanced at Chief Abrams. "Chief?"

Chief Abrams walked over and leaned against the bar.

"This is one of those parts of the job I hate," he said. "I'm sorry, Walter, but I need to bring the state police in. They're going to talk with you, and you'll need to explain everything that happened in the hunting camp. Then they're probably going to arrest you and decide if they want to charge you with involuntary manslaughter."

"But it was an accident," Coke Bottle said, his eyes pleading.

"That's why it's called involuntary, Walter," Chief Abrams said.

"Oh. If I get convicted, what am I looking at?"

"Probably at least a year, plus probation," Chief Abrams said. "But if you get a good lawyer, you might be able to plea it down."

"I can't afford a good lawyer."

"Leave that one to me, Walter," Rooster said, patting him on the shoulder. "Now just sit there quietly and wait for the state police."

Rooster waved his finger at Rocco to indicate another round of drinks. Chief Abrams walked into the dining room to make his phone call. Fifteen minutes later, two state policemen arrived, and they huddled briefly with Chief Abrams. Then they approached Walter, and he slowly got down off the barstool and put his hands behind his back.

"I'm so sorry, Rooster," he said, looking back over his shoulder as he was led away in handcuffs.

"Yeah, me too," Rooster whispered, then tossed back his drink. "I'll have another, Rocco."

"Are you going to be okay?" I said, sitting back down.

"I'll be fine," Rooster said. "At least now I know what happened and don't have to worry about trying to track the killers down."

"Rooster, I'm going to pretend you didn't say that," Chief Abrams said, then looked at me. "How the heck did you figure it out?"

"I saw how he reacted to something at the memorial service and just put it together," I said.

"Impressive," he said.

"Thanks, but I don't feel very good about it," I said. "Look, I'm worn out, so I think I'm going to head home. Unless you've got any other questions for me."

"Just one," Chief Abrams deadpanned. "Could you tell me what tonight's specials are?"

Chapter 21

"Schizophrenic, huh?" Josie said as she stared out the front window of the diner.

I slowly lowered my menu and peered over the top at her.

"Is that a self-diagnosis, or the prevailing professional opinion?"

"Funny. I'm talking about the weather," she said, then transitioned into mock humility. "But if I were to describe my own personality, I think the word to use would be *delightful*. What do you think?"

"I'd ask for a second opinion if I were you," I said, raising my menu.

But as far as the weather was concerned, Josie was right. Unlike yesterday's cold rain and wind that made the adventurous long for the sun and old bones ache, Mother Nature had turned the page and delivered a cloudless blue sky and temperatures in the seventies.

"If we have time after lunch, I thought we'd grab the dogs and take the boat out," Josie said.

"We better hurry," I said, setting the menu down. "It's supposed to snow later today."

"How is that possible?" she said, again staring out the window. "Here he comes."

Rooster entered the diner and spotted us right away.

"Sorry I'm a bit late," he said. "Titan decided he couldn't pass up the opportunity to do battle with a porcupine."

"Uh-oh. He didn't get hurt, did he?" Josie said.

"No, but I can't say the same thing for the porcupine," Rooster said.

"Did Titan kill it?" I said, grimacing.

"Nah, it managed to escape. But I doubt if it plans on returning to my garage anytime soon."

Our waitress approached, and we all ordered the corned beef hash. She poured coffee for Rooster and topped ours off, then left.

"Well, Chief was right," Rooster said. "I just got a call from Walter's lawyer, and they're charging him with involuntary manslaughter."

"I'm sorry, Rooster," I said.

"He'll be fine. The lawyer is pretty sure that, given the circumstances and the fact that Chef Claire decided not to press charges for stealing the dogs, he'll get probation."

"How long?" I said.

"Three to five years. And maybe six months of house arrest thrown in for good measure."

"Are you okay with that?" I said.

"As long as he doesn't spend the six months in my house, I'm fine with it," Rooster said, adding cream to his coffee. "I told the lawyer to make sure the judge convinces my cousin to spend his probation under the sunny skies of Florida."

"I wish I could say I was sorry to see him leave," I said.

Josie's phone rang, and she answered it on the second ring.

"This is Josie. What? Ah, geez," she said, shaking her head. "Okay, get prepped for surgery, and I'll be there in five minutes. Thanks, Jill."

"What is it?" I said.

"Mrs. Frey's lab puppy just ate a scouring pad."

"The kind you clean pots and pans with?" Rooster said.

"That's the one," she said. "And a fresh one right out of the box, too. That means in addition to having to swallowed chunks of wire, she might have also poisoned herself."

"You can't wait for her to just pass it?" Rooster said.

"No, I need to do everything possible right away to make sure the cleaning solution on those pads doesn't kill her, and if those metal shards start working their way through her digestive track, it could get ugly in a hurry. I'll see you later."

We watched Josie dash out of the diner and speed away in her car.

"That dog's in good hands," Rooster said.

"Yeah, it sure is," I said. "Well, I guess I'm going to need a ride home after breakfast."

"Couldn't get yours to cooperate this morning?" Rooster said, laughing.

"Actually, it's still drying out from yesterday."

"What is it with you and that SUV?"

"It's a long story," I said. "And it's probably quite silly when you boil it all down."

"I don't think it's silly," Rooster said.

"You don't even know the story."

"No, but I know you. And even when you go off and do something goofy, you always have your reasons," he said, taking a sip of coffee before continuing. "It's about your dad, isn't it?"

"Yeah," I said, starting to choke up. "How did you know that?"

"Just a lucky guess. You know," he said, leaning back and draping an arm across the top of the booth. "I remember the day your dad bought that SUV. We walked into the dealership, and he took one look at it and bought it on the spot. He didn't even test drive it. Which I thought was crazy. But I guess your dad knew quality when he saw it, huh?"

"You were there with him?"

"I was. You were around twelve at the time if I remember."

"Thirteen. He died six months after he bought it," I said, tearing up.

"Yeah. Bad day," he whispered.

"I had to wait three years before I could even drive it. Now, it's the last tangible thing I have that keeps him fresh in my mind. I can't bear to get rid of it."

"Who says you have to get rid of it? People have been known to own more than one car," he said.

"I can't leave a rusting pile of junk sitting outside my house," I said. "It's not fair to my neighbors, and they'd have every right to start complaining. And they'd be complaining to the mayor, who just happens to be my mother in case you forgot."

"Yeah, she wouldn't appreciate that very much," he said. "But if your father was here, you know what he'd do, right?"

"Kick my butt for driving around in such an unsafe vehicle?"

"You bet he would."

"I can't get rid of it, Rooster."

"Then don't. Tell you what, we'll stash it away in my storage garage, and you can come visit it anytime you like. We'll even make sure to keep it running so every once in a while you can take it out for a drive. On a day when the sun's out."

"I can't believe I didn't think of doing something like that," I said, frowning. "It's such a simple solution."

"That's because you've been overthinking it for a couple of years, and now you've got yourself completely wrapped around the axle. Just like you're doing with trying to figure out who stole Chef Claire's dogs."

"Well, that mystery should be revealed tonight."

"Maybe," Rooster said, glancing off into the distance before focusing back on me. "But we've got all day to kill before then."

"What? You think I should go car shopping today?"

"No, I think *we* should go car shopping. Right after breakfast."

"I don't know, Rooster."

"Why not?"

"Because… Actually, I don't have a good reason."

"It doesn't matter. I wasn't going to listen to it anyway," he said, grinning.

Our waitress arrived with our breakfast. She glanced around the table then looked at me.

"Where's Josie?"

"She had an emergency surgery to take care of," I said.

"What should I do with all this food?"

"Just box it up, and I'll take it with me. Thanks, Sally."

We ate our breakfast in relative silence, then headed to the Inn so I could grab my checkbook. I stopped by the surgery area to say a quick hello to Josie and Jill. They barely looked up when I popped my head in, and when I caught a glimpse of what they were doing, I made a beeline for the reception area. I touched base with Sammy and left Josie's breakfast with him. Then we headed for a dealership about thirty miles away whose owner was a good friend of Rooster and my mom.

Ten minutes into the drive, a thought popped into my head.

"This is the same dealership where my dad bought the SUV, isn't it?"

"It is," Rooster said, staring out through the windshield. "Man, it feels like spring today."

"It's supposed to snow later."

"Lucky for you, you'll be inside a warm and toasty new car," he said, glancing over at me.

We drove for another ten minutes, and then a lightbulb went off.

"Rooster?"

"Yeah."

"My mother put you up to this, didn't she?"

"Yup," he said without taking his eyes off the road.

"She called you yesterday right after I left the funeral home."

"Yup."

"Let me guess. She said something like *Rooster, I've just about reached the end of my tether with Suzy's car.*"

Rooster laughed and nodded.

"That was good. You've got her down."

"Unbelievable," I said, shaking my head. "What a piece of work."

"She does work in mysterious ways."

"I can't believe the way she keeps sticking her nose where it doesn't belong," I snapped.

"Uh, Suzy, I hope you don't mind my pointing out the rather ironic nature of your last statement."

"Yeah, good point," I said, nodding. "But still."

"Well, if it makes you feel any better, this whole thing about the new car was kind of a group vote. And it was unanimous."

"You're ganging up on me?"

"Only for your own good," he said, turning into the dealership and parking right in front of the entrance. "You ready?"

"I suppose."

"Let's go have a look at what they've got in the showroom," he said, heading for the entrance.

I followed him inside, glanced around, and then saw it sitting right in the center of the room. I walked up to it and gently ran my hand over the hood. It was forest green with tan leather seats, and I couldn't take my eyes off it.

"Hop in," Rooster said, opening the driver door.

I did, and I was immediately enveloped by the plush seat. I looked at the dashboard and decided the SUV probably contained more technology than some of the earlier space flights. I glanced over my shoulder and nodded at the ample room it provided for the dogs. I hopped out of the vehicle and did a couple of slow laps around it.

"There they are," the owner said as he approached. "How are you doing, Rooster?"

"Hey, Roger. I'm good."

Roger looked me with a big smile on his face.

"Finally," he said, laughing and spreading his arms wide. "It's a miracle."

"Hi, Roger. Yes, I've succumbed to public pressure."

"What do you think?" Roger said.

"It's perfect," I said.

"Then hop in, and we'll take it out for a little test drive."

"No," I said, glancing at the vehicle, then back at Rooster. I shook my head. "That won't be necessary."

"Well, all right then," Roger said, clapping his hands. "Let me go get the paperwork started. If you want to bring your trade-in around to the back, we'll get a number worked up for it."

"No, I won't be doing a trade-in."

"Even easier," Roger said, now beaming. "It's such a pleasure doing business with a woman who knows what she wants."

I put my hands on my hips and stared at him.

"Tell me something, Roger. Do you get the same pleasure dealing with men who know what they want?"

"I'm sorry, Suzy. I misspoke. I wasn't trying to make any gender comparisons," he said, backtracking as fast as his little legs could carry him. "I apologize."

"Don't worry about it, Roger," I said, glancing at the window sticker that outlined the vehicle's features and price. "Just knock three grand off the sticker price, and I'll write you a check."

"Three grand?" he said, giving me a look like I'd just shot his dog. "Geez, Suzy. I don't think I can do that."

"That's okay, Roger," I said. "I'm sure I can find it online."

Roger's smile faded a bit, and he stared at me.

"You really are your mother's daughter, aren't you?"

"Yeah. But try not to spread it around. So, I'm assuming you can do the three grand?"

"Yeah, I can do the three grand," he said. "I'll be back in a few minutes. Right after I stop the bleeding."

He walked away, and I refocused on my new car. I began imagining myself behind the wheel, and then yet another thought popped into my head.

"Rooster?"

"Yeah?"

"My mother called Roger this morning and told him to park it right here, didn't she?"

"Actually, that was my idea," he said.

"I see. And you thought you'd take a quick trip down memory lane over breakfast before we came out here?"

"No, that was your mother's idea."

"You do know how incredibly manipulative that was, right?"

"I do," Rooster said, nodding. "But we did good, didn't we?"

"Yeah, you did good."

Chapter 22

The weatherman had been right, and around five in the afternoon, it started snowing. And just so we didn't miss her latest reminder that winter was just around the corner, Mother Nature included strong winds out of the north and a forty-degree temperature drop. On my drive home, I'd been forced to close the sunroof as well as turn on the heater as the cold front swept in.

But the SUV hugged the highway like I held puppies, and I knew that my dad would be happy to know that I was now both safe and comfortable whenever I was on the road. Once I got home, I kept sneaking peeks out at the window at the sparkling SUV parked in the driveway and, at times, felt giddy. I'd never had a brand new car before and was beginning to understand what all the fuss was about. It would take me forever to figure out how all the different buttons and features worked, and I knew that the new car smell would soon be replaced by the scent of musty dog. But I had all the time in the world, and the dogs were more than welcome to make themselves comfortable.

We fed and let the dogs outside earlier than usual, and by six-thirty, they were all back in their condos and settled in. Chief Abrams and Jackson arrived at the same time shortly after that, and we convened in the condo area to discuss our plans for the evening.

"The state police actually said they didn't want to help out?" I said to Chief Abrams.

"They certainly did. And my request was met with a rather rude rejection. The new commander of the station is a real tough nut to crack. And I think he might be a bit of head case as well. He seems to get that crazed commando look whenever anybody disagrees with him. I think I got out of there at the right time. He's a lot different from Shorty."

Chief Abrams had been one of the state police lead detectives for years before leaving to become our new chief of police. Shorty, recently retired, was the former commander and someone Chief Abrams had worked with for years.

"I can't believe he wasn't interested," I said. "What did he say?"

"He said that if he wanted to send his staff on wild-goose chases, he'd just wait for hunting season," Chief Abrams said.

"That was kind of rude," I said.

"But he did say that if our *idiotic idea* somehow happened to pan out, he'd be more than happy to swing by and arrest somebody."

"I don't think I like this guy," I said.

"Join the club," Chief Abrams said. "So I called Jackson, and he kindly agreed to help us out."

"At least it gets me out of the store for a while," Jackson said. "This afternoon I caught myself talking to a box of tomatoes. I think I'm starting to lose it."

"Thanks for coming," Josie said, patting his hand. "And I'm sure the tomatoes understand."

"Are you going to be like this all night?" Jackson said.

"Tired and grumpy?" Josie said. "Yeah, I like the odds."

"Thanks for the warning," Jackson said. "What do you need me to do?"

"We'd like you to handle the outside perimeter," I said.

Josie snorted. I ignored her, but Jackson reacted.

"Outside perimeter?" he said.

"She wants you to walk around the fence line of the dog's play area all night," Josie said.

"In this weather?" Jackson said.

"Why not?" I said, shrugging. "You're dressed for it."

"Gee, Suzy, that sounds like a lot of fun. And the state police didn't want to join in? I'm shocked." he said. "Maybe we should do it in shifts. You know, take turns handling the *outside perimeter*."

"Well, don't look at me," Josie said, yawning. "The only reason I'm down here is because I need to keep a close eye on a Lab puppy that just came out of a very tough surgery."

"How is she doing?" I said.

"She should be fine," Josie said. "But if Mrs. Frey hadn't called when she did, I don't think the little girl would have made it. That reminds me, we need to check the house to make sure we don't have anything like those scouring pads stored where Al can get at them."

"Chef Claire already did it this afternoon," I said. "We're good."

"So, getting back to my idea about taking turns handling the outside?" Jackson said.

I looked at Chief Abrams who nodded.

"Okay," I said. "I don't mind. You take the first shift, Jackson. One of us will relieve you at ten."

"Ten? That's three hours," Jackson said, frowning. "I'm gonna freeze my butt off."

"Oh, you'll be fine," I said, waving his protest away.

"The tomatoes are looking pretty good right about now, huh?" Josie said.

"We should probably come up with some sort of signal," Jackson said. "I've been working on some bird calls in my spare time."

All three of us stared at him.

"We really need to get you a girlfriend, Jackson," I said.

"Tell me about it," he said. "I've got my Snowy Owl call down pretty good. How about if I hoot three times if I see anybody coming?"

"Sure, sure," I said. "Or you could just text me."

Embarrassed, Jackson nodded and checked his phone, then headed out the back door.

"See you at ten," I said. "And don't forget to text me if you see anything."

I closed the door but left it unlocked.

"I'm sorry I'm a bit late," Rooster said, walking from the reception area into the condo area.

Titan, his German shepherd, stood at his side and looked around at us.

"No, you're right on time," I said, kneeling down to greet the shepherd. "How are you doing, Titan? Rooster, he looks great."

"Thanks," he said, beaming at the dog. "I gave him a light supper just to make sure he's got a bit of an appetite in case anybody shows up. How does the new car handle?"

"It's amazing. And thanks again for the nudge."

"Happy to do it, but you know who you need to thank."

"Don't remind me."

"Okay, Chief. What do you need from me?"

"Hopefully nothing," Chief Abrams said. "Provide a little muscle if necessary. And if you could get Titan to snarl and growl at the right time, it might encourage them to talk."

"So, we're just going to sit here in the dark and wait until somebody shows up?" Rooster said.

"Pretty much," I said. "But we were able to come up with a spot near the supply closet where we can keep a light on without it being visible outside."

"That's great," Rooster said. "I'm glad I remembered to bring the cribbage board. How about two dollars a point?"

"Sure, why not?" I said, laughing. "I've spent a ton of money today. I wouldn't mind winning back some of it."

"Fat chance," Rooster said, setting up the board and handing a deck of cards to Chief Abrams.

"Where's the lady dog judge?" Rooster said.

"Alexandra's up at the house with her two Goldens keeping an eye on our guys," Josie said, glancing at her cards.

"How's she doing today?" Chief Abrams said, also studying his cards.

"She's been pretty quiet," Josie said. "And still pretty rattled about the idea of somebody trying to kill her."

"Can't blame her for that," I said, setting my phone on the table. "My cards don't look very good."

"They look okay from here," Josie said.

"Stop peeking at my cards."

"I wasn't peeking. They just happened to be in my line of sight."

"Are we going to play cards, or are you two going to pick at each other all night?" Rooster said.

"Probably a lot of both," Josie said, playing a card. "Fifteen for two."

Over the next two hours, Rooster's grin grew wider as his winnings increased. By the time he was up four hundred, it looked like he was about to break into his happy dance. And despite my constant checking, I didn't receive any texts from Jackson and the time passed quickly.

Just after nine, I was shuffling the cards when I heard a noise near the back door and paused.

"Shhh," I said, flipping the light off. "Did you hear that?"

"Yup," Rooster said.

In the darkness, Rooster was hard to see as he stood and gave Titan a soft whistle. Then I heard him tiptoe his way toward the back door. Titan's toenails clicked softly on the polished cement floor.

"Easy, Titan," Rooster whispered.

Despite the potential danger, knowing that I was here with Rooster and Chief Abrams, I felt a sense of calmness come over me. Then I remembered an important detail.

"Rooster, wait," I said in a controlled whisper.

"Stay there," he whispered back.

Then he heard the back door squeak as it began to open and his voice got loud.

"Get him, Titan!"

The shepherd growled and snapped his jaws as he bounced through the door on his way out. Seconds later, we heard screams rising above the dog's vicious guttural growls. I got up and started to head for the main light switch, stumbled over Chief Abrams' chair, but eventually managed to get the lights on as the screams from outside the door increased.

"What the heck?" Rooster said, staring down at the man Titan had by the ankle. "What are doing here, Jackson?"

"At the moment, fighting for my life," Jackson said, doing his best to fend off the shepherd that seemed determined to remove the leg from its socket.

"Titan. Release," Rooster snapped.

The dog immediately let go of Jackson's leg but continued to hover and snarl.

"Titan. Sit."

The dog again complied and sat down at Rooster's feet and replaced the snarl with a low growl.

"Jackson, I'm so sorry," I said, racing outside. "Are you okay?"

Jackson sat up and removed his boot to examine his foot.

"I think I'm okay," he said, pulling his boot back on. "Lucky for me I'm wearing my winter boots."

"Lucky for you, Rooster didn't train him to go for the face," Josie said, shaking her head. "What were you thinking trying to walk in without letting us know?"

"Well, just before I got attacked, I was thinking about how bad I needed to pee," Jackson said, standing up. "But I think we can cross that one off the list."

"I'm sorry, Jackson," I said. "I probably should have mentioned that Rooster was bringing Titan with him."

"Ya' think?" Jackson snapped.

"And it probably would have helped if you had told me that Jackson was out there," Rooster said, glaring at me. "Titan could have done some real damage."

"Yeah," I said, embarrassed. "I kind of whiffed on that one."

"Come inside, Jackson. I want to take a look at that foot," Josie said.

"Okay, thanks," he said, glancing at Titan then at Rooster. "Should I pet him on my way past?"

"You might want to wait a few minutes," Rooster said, holding the growling Titan by his collar.

Jackson carefully limped his way around the dog and came inside. Josie examined his foot and didn't find any damage. But the boot had certainly seen better days.

"Well, I guess it's nice to see Titan that hasn't lost his edge," I said, trying to lighten the mood.

"Maybe he can give you a few tips," Rooster said, still grumpy.

"I said I was sorry," I said. "How many times do you want me to apologize?"

"Just get started, and we'll let you know when to stop," Rooster said.

"It's really not my fault," I said, pouting.

"Disagree," all four said in unison.

Chapter 23

Right after breakfast the next morning, we helped Alexandra load her car. I held the door open, and Lucky and Lucy hopped effortlessly into the backseat. Alexandra closed the hatchback and glanced around deep in thought.

"I have the strangest feeling that I'm forgetting something," she said.

"Car keys, wallet, and your dogs," Josie said. "That's the important stuff. Anything else can be easily replaced."

Alexandra laughed and gave Josie a warm hug.

"You're too much," she said, then frowned again. "I know I've forgotten something. And it's driving me crazy."

"If we find anything, we'll mail it you," I said.

"Thanks. If you do, please send it to my sister's place in Saratoga Springs. My husband's upcoming travel schedule is very heavy, so I'll be staying with her until we get all this trouble sorted out. You'll find the address on her website."

"Got it," I said, hugging her. "Thanks for everything, Alexandra."

"It was my pleasure," she said. "I'm sorry you got dragged into my mess. And I'm especially sorry that all your efforts last night didn't bear any fruit."

"Don't worry about it," I said. "If it had, Josie would have just eaten it all."

"You were so sure they were going to show up," Alexandra said.

"Yeah, well, it's not the first time I've been wrong about something like that," I said, shrugging. "But it was worth a shot."

"Well, I appreciate all the effort."

"Are you sure you're going to be okay?" I said.

"I'll be fine," Alexandra said.

"I wish you'd reconsider our suggestion about hiring some security people to keep an eye on you."

"I'll think about it," she said, climbing into the driver seat. "But since they didn't show up last night, maybe they've lost interest."

"Maybe. But just promise us that you'll be extra careful," Josie said.

"I will," she said, starting the car. "I need to get on the road if I'm going to get Lucky to his appointment on time."

"Have fun, Lucky," Josie said, reaching through the window to stroke his head.

"Stay in touch, and I hope we see you back here for next year's show," I said.

"I would love that. Bye now."

She waved and headed down the driveway. We watched until the car disappeared from view and then started to walk toward the Inn.

"She's such a nice woman," I said.

"Yes, she is. But I can't decide if she's oblivious to the danger she's in, or is just choosing to ignore it and hope it goes away."

"Yeah, I was wondering the same thing," I said. "Would it be too much for us to call the people putting on the dog show in Massachusetts and give them a heads up?"

Josie thought about it for a few seconds, then shook her head.

"I think that might be crossing the line," she said. "Alexandra's a big girl, and, when you boil it all down, it's really none of our business."

"That sounds a bit harsh," I said.

"Yeah, it probably does. But that doesn't make it any less true. Besides, she'll be staying with her sister the rest of the week, and her husband is going to meet her at the show. As long as she pays attention to what's going on around her, she should be fine, right?"

"I guess," I said, glancing up at the sky. "I wish this weather would make up its mind. Schizophrenic is definitely the right word for it. It's supposed to go back into the sixties this afternoon."

"But the wind is supposed to kick up, and it'll probably be too cold to take the boat out. But I wouldn't mind tooling around later in your new car."

"It's nice, isn't it?" I said, staring with pride at the SUV.

"It certainly is. And I won't have to worry about getting soaked or falling through the floorboards every time I get in it."

"Don't start. Did I tell you the owner of the dealership said that it was a pleasure dealing with a woman who actually knew what she wanted?"

"I hope you had the appropriate gender conversation with him," she said, laughing.

"I did."

"And?"

"And he agreed to knock three grand off the sticker price."

"Well done. I hope you handled the negotiation in a very manly fashion."

"I did," I said, giving her a quick smile before heading back inside my head. "I still can't believe they didn't show up last night."

"Jackson's screams probably scared them off."

"Yeah, that could have been a very bad situation," I said, still cringing every time I thought about the dog shaking Jackson's leg like it was a chew toy.

"Rooster needs to put up a sign on his dock next summer," Josie said. "Something like; *Complain about my gas prices at your own risk.*"

"I was so sure they were in that storage area in the arena."

"Suzy, it's way too early in the day for you to start obsessing."

"Sure, sure," I said. "I was absolutely certain they were there."

"I know you were. But I was never quite convinced," Josie said.

"Really? You should have said something."

Josie stopped walking and stared at me in disbelief.

"You're unbelievable," she said.

"What?"

"You don't remember my rather vociferous protests at the time?"

"I thought you were just demonstrating another aspect of your *delightful* personality."

"Okay, Dr. Freud," she said. "I'm done with this conversation. I'm going to head inside and talk to the wall in my office."

"I think I'm in a slump," I said.

"And you're trying to think your way out of it?"

"Yes."

"Well, do me a favor and try to do it without talking."

I held the door open for her and we went to check in on the Lab puppy that was sleeping peacefully on a thick bed in one of the condos. Josie stepped inside and knelt down and scratched one of the puppy's ears. She opened her eyes and began licking Josie's hand.

"So, you're feeling a bit better today, huh?" she said, gently rolling the puppy onto her back to examine the bandage and stitches. "What a good girl."

"How does she look?" I said, peering inside the condo.

"She's going to be just fine," Josie said, climbing to her feet.

"Now that is the definition of delightful," I said, staring down at the Lab that had rolled over on her own and gone back to sleep.

Josie laughed and playfully waved me away as she headed for her office. I continued along the line of condos to say good morning to the rest of our dogs and immediately began to feel better.

Chapter 24

Stuffed to the gills, I pushed my plate away and groaned. I grabbed my glass of carbonated water, took a long drink, and leaned back in my chair. I gently pressed my hand against my stomach then burped loudly. Josie and Chef Claire both stared at me.

"Really? At the dinner table?" Josie said. "Very ladylike."

"Pardon me," I said. "Sorry, but I couldn't help it."

"If your mother could only see you now," Chef Claire said, laughing.

"This is all your fault," I said to Chef Claire.

"How is your complete lack of self-control my fault?" she said, also pushing her plate away. "I somehow managed to stop after two helpings."

"You know what always happens when you make that gumbo."

"Yeah. You eat too much, and then you whine," Chef Claire said.

"I'm not whining," I said, taking another gulp of my fizzy water. "By the way, it was delicious. Thank you."

"What happened to your pre-Grand Cayman fitness campaign?" Josie said. "You've only got three weeks left."

"I'm still on it," I said, protesting weakly. "I've been walking every day."

"Yeah, to the fridge," Josie deadpanned.

"Shut up."

"It's my turn to do dishes," Josie said. "Why don't you guys get settled in and see if you can find a movie worth watching?"

Josie carried a stack of plates into the kitchen as Chef Claire and I headed for the living room. The dogs greeted us, and Chloe hopped up onto one of the couches and waited for me to join her. I tossed a couple of pieces of wood on the fire then stretched out. Chloe draped herself across my legs.

"Mama ate too much," I said, stroking her head.

"Here's one about a family that inherits a haunted house then starts mysteriously disappearing one by one," Chef Claire said, holding the remote as she reviewed the channel menu.

"That works for me."

I closed my eyes and was about to doze off when Josie came in the living room and stretched out on the floor to wrestle with Captain. Then she sat with her back against the couch and the dog draped across her lap.

"Is ever going to stop growing?" I said, admiring the massive Newfie.

"I think he's almost done," Josie said, maneuvering some of Captain's weight off her legs. "And it's about time. He's been at a hundred and forty pounds for a couple weeks now."

"And thinks he's still a puppy," I said. "Don't you, Captain?"

He looked up at me and thumped his tail against the floor.

"You guys ready to start the movie?" Chef Claire said.

"Could you put it on the local news for a minute?" Josie said. "I want to check the weather. They're talking about rain tomorrow, and we might want to adjust our morning schedule. I'd love to avoid having to deal with another bunch of muddy dogs if at all possible."

"You and me both," I said, remembering the rainstorm the day of the memorial service that had turned the outside play area into a muddy quagmire for a couple of days.

Chef Claire changed channels, and we watched the end of the sports report. Then the commercials started.

"We've got a few minutes before the weather comes on," Chef Claire said. "Let's see what's going on in the rest of the world."

She changed channels to a national news network, and we immediately saw dozens of flashing lights and cop cars surrounding a rainy intersection.

"Oh, no," Chef Claire said. "Something's happened."

"Terror attack?" I said.

"Let's hope not," Josie said.

We listened carefully as we tried to pick up the thread of the conversation. When we heard the reporter with a thick Boston accent mention a dog show, we all sat upright and looked at each other with stunned expressions before refocusing on the TV.

"Here's what we know, Mary," the on the scene reporter said as the water poured off the hood of his rain slicker. *"About an hour ago, renowned breeder and dog show judge, Alexandra Vincent, and her husband, Harold, were crossing a street near their hotel when they were struck and killed by a hit and run driver."*

"Oh, no," Josie whispered.

"I can't believe it," I said, immediately tearing up.

"Mrs. Vincent was in town to judge a dog show being held this weekend in Brookline and the accident occurred just after 8 PM local time when the couple was apparently on their way to a nearby restaurant when a car roared through a red light at a high rate of speed. Police sources say they were both probably killed instantly. Since it has been raining most of the day, foot traffic on the street was very light, and the police have only identified two witnesses. So far, they have been unable to provide any details other than saying that everything happened very fast and that the vehicle never slowed down even after striking the couple. As such, both the driver and the vehicle involved remain unknown at this time. And we've also just learned that the Vincent's prized dogs, two Golden Retrievers that are frequently featured in various magazines and seen in numerous television commercials, are missing."

Chef Claire lowered the volume, and we sat in stunned silence for several seconds. All three of us fought back the tears as we tried to process what we'd just heard.

"A hit and run accident?" Josie said. "I'm not buying it."

"It wasn't an accident," I said. "If it were an accident, the dogs wouldn't be missing."

"I guess she didn't take our advice to hire some security," Chef Claire said. "I can't believe she's gone."

"What do you think?" Josie said.

"I think we should have pushed her a bit harder to take the threat seriously," I said, wiping my eyes.

"Don't even try to go there, Suzy," Josie said, also fighting her emotions. "This is not our fault. And it was a hit and run. How would you ever prepare for something like that?"

"I know. But still."

"What should we do?" Chef Claire said.

"What can we do?" I said. "Apart from finding out where the service is going to be held and send flowers."

I exhaled loudly and Chloe, sensing my sadness, nuzzled my arm. My phone buzzed, and I answered it immediately.

"This is Suzy. Hey, Chief. Yeah, we just watched it." I rubbed my forehead as I listened closely. "Thanks, Chief. Yeah, we'll be fine." I tossed my phone aside. "When Chief heard what happened, he called an old buddy who's with the Boston police to see if he could get any more details."

"And?" Josie said.

"It was pretty much what we saw on the news. Dark, rainy, empty streets. Nobody saw anything. Chief's buddy said that they would have to get very lucky identifying who hit them."

"They're going to get away with murder?" Chef Claire said.

"It certainly looks that way," I said.

"Did he mention the dogs?" Josie said.

"Just that they were missing from the hotel," I said.

"After they ran them down, they went back to the hotel for the dogs?" Josie said.

"Maybe. Or they split up, and one drove the car while the other stole the dogs," I said, shrugging.

"This is too weird," Chef Claire said. "I know those dogs are amazing, but who would kill two people just to get their hands on them?"

"I have no idea," I said, wiping my eyes with a tissue. "But I think we've seen the last of Lucky and Lucy." Then I caught the wide-eyed stares they were giving me. "No, I don't mean that. I'm sure they're not going to hurt them, but I doubt if we'll see them in any more dog shows or on TV."

"But they'll still be breeding them," Josie said.

"Yeah, that's my guess. And Lucky will be fine since he's a male. But I don't like Lucy's chances once she's all used up and can't produce any more litters."

"Is there any way we could track them down?" Chef Claire said.

"Geez, that's a real long shot. We eventually located the owner of that Dandie Dinmont we found, but we had to get very lucky in the process. And there are only a couple of hundred

Dandie puppies born each year. There are over fifty thousand new Goldens annually."

"At least," Josie said, nodding. "We'd never find them. I wouldn't even know where to start. Especially since the people who stole them will be doing everything they can to stay out of sight."

"This is so sad. And just think about how close I came to losing Al and Dente," Chef Claire said, glancing around. "Hey, wait a minute. Where's Al?"

Chef Claire hopped off the couch and looked around the room before she spotted Al behind my couch.

"What have you got there, Al?" Chef Claire said.

I glanced over the back of the couch and did my best not to laugh. Al had a leather bag tucked under his front legs and was grasping it with both front paws as he chewed his way through the thick strap. He paused long enough to look up at us with a guilty look on his face, then went back to work on the strap.

"No," Chef Claire said, snatching the bag out of Al's paws. "Bad dog, Al. Bad dog."

"Say it like you mean it," Josie said, laughing.

"I'm trying," Chef Claire said, giggling. "But did you see the look he gave me?"

"You're a soft touch," Josie said, then looked at Al. "What are we going to do with you?"

"I'm sorry, Josie," Chef Claire said. "I'll pay you for the bag."

"It's not my bag," she said, shaking her head.

"It's not mine," I said when Chef Claire looked at me. "I bet it's Alexandra's. The day she left, she said she was sure she forgot something."

"I wonder where he found it," Chef Claire said.

"I just cleaned the guest bedroom yesterday," I said. "But I suppose it could have been under the bed."

"That would explain the dust bunnies," Josie said.

"Don't start."

Chef Claire examined the contents of the bag and extracted a thick folder she took a quick glance at.

"It's hers. This folder is all dog show stuff."

"Just toss it on the table and on Monday we'll send it off to Alexandra's sister in Saratoga," I said.

Chef Claire set the bag down on the dining room table. Al eyed the bag carefully, then looked up at Chef Claire and cocked his head.

"Al, don't even think about it," Chef Claire said, glancing down at the dog.

Al woofed once at her, then trotted back into the living room and pounced on Dente. Within seconds, they were rolling around on the floor.

"What a little monster," Chef Claire said, returning to the couch. "Do you think he'll ever grow out of it?"

"Apart from the chewing," Josie said. "I sure hope not."

"Yeah, he is pretty special, isn't he?"

We watched Al turn his attention to Captain who was still draped over Josie's legs and sound asleep. Al grabbed one of Captain's ears and tugged at it. Captain slowly opened his eyes, then draped a paw over Al and pinned him to the floor. Al struggled free, snarled playfully at Captain, then trotted off and returned a few minutes later with one of Josie's shoes. He stood a few feet away from her, just out of reach, and taunted her as he gently held the shoe in his mouth.

"Drop it, Al," Josie said, then started laughing. "Did you see that? He just shook his head at me." She composed herself, then said sternly, "Don't make me get my *scissors*, Al."

Al immediately dropped the shoe and stretched out at Chef Claire's feet with his head propped up on his front paws.

"Wow, that was pretty amazing. When did you teach him that?" Chef Claire said.

"We've been working on it for a couple of days," Josie said. "I got the idea from Alexandra when I saw how Lucky responded to the word clinic."

"Only a couple of days?" I said. "Smart dog."

"Yes, he is," Josie said. "And a little nervous."

Chapter 25

I was chatting with Sammy and Jill at reception bright and early on Monday morning when the front door opened and Rooster entered, trailed closely by Titan. Both of them had gotten drenched on the short walk from the parking lot, and Titan was limping and favoring his left front paw. Titan shook and sprayed water in several directions. Rooster didn't shake, but a small pool of water did collect at his feet. I tossed Rooster a towel expecting him to use it on himself, but he started drying the German shepherd with it. Then he glanced around looking for somewhere to put the soaked towel, and I pointed at a bin we'd put in the corner.

"Sorry about the mess," Rooster said, tossing the towel into the bin.

"Don't worry about it," I said, kneeling down to pet Titan. "After two days of this, we're getting pretty used to it."

"Speak for yourself," Sammy said, swabbing the floor with a mop.

"I think Titan nicked his front paw on something," Rooster said, stepping to one side to give Sammy more room. "I couldn't find anything, but he's been favoring it since last night."

"Poor guy," I said, stroking the shepherd's head. "Jill, can you text Josie and ask her to come out?"

Jill sent the message, and Josie soon emerged from the condo area scowling.

"Anybody want to buy a hundred and forty pound Newfie?" she said. "He's going cheap today."

"He rolled around in the mud again, didn't he?" I said.

"Oh, yeah," she said. "So much for the bath I gave him last night."

"I told you to wait until it stopped raining. What can I say? He's a water dog."

"More like a mud dog at the moment," Josie said. "Hey, Rooster. How are you doing?"

"I'm good. But I think Titan picked something up in his front paw. I tried to take a look, but he wouldn't let me anywhere near it."

"I'll take a look at it on one condition, Rooster," Josie said. "After I start the exam, you have to agree not to yell, *Go get her!*"

Rooster chuckled and gently thumped Titan on the side. Titan wagged his tail at the love taps and stared up at Rooster.

"Yeah," he said, frowning. "That could have ended badly. Fortunately, he listens to me."

"Jill, let's put Titan in exam room two," Josie said.

"You're not going to have to put him under, are you?" Rooster said.

"Not as long as he doesn't try to bite me," Josie said.

"Then maybe I should be in there with you," he said.

"Great minds think alike," Josie said, heading for the exam room.

After they had entered the exam room, I headed for the reception desk to continue reviewing the day's schedule with Sammy.

"It's pretty light today," Sammy said. "We've got a couple of boarders coming in this afternoon, and Josie has three annuals scheduled. But that's about it. Oh, I almost forgot. Jerome just called. He's in town and is stopping by in a bit."

"Sounds good. We'll need every spare minute we can find to stay on top of the mud," I said, glancing out at the rain that continued to pound the ground.

"You know, I was thinking we might want to consider putting up a covered section over part of the play area where the dogs could do their business," Sammy said. "It wouldn't have to be big or that expensive, and it might cut down on the mud factor when it gets like this."

"I like it, Sammy," I said, nodding. "Sketch something up, and we'll discuss it with Josie."

"Will do," he said, then cleared his throat. "There's something else I'd like to discuss with you."

"Sure. What is it?"

Sammy reached into his pocket and pulled out a small box. He opened it and held it up for me to see.

"Sammy, I never knew you cared," I deadpanned.

"Funny. It's for Jill."

"I know who it's for, Sammy," I said, laughing. "It's a gorgeous ring."

"Thanks," he said, beaming. "I'm going to propose tonight."

"Congratulations. Where are you going to do it?"

"Over dinner at our place," he said. "I'm a lousy cook, but I thought the ring might help her get past the burnt chicken."

"Why don't you take her to C's?"

"I would, but I'm a little short on cash at the moment. That ring set me back a bit."

"My treat," I said, smiling at him. "Think of it as a pre-wedding gift."

"Geez, Suzy," he said, frowning. "I don't know. You already do so much for us."

"Not nearly as much as you and Jill do for us, Sammy. You better put that away before she comes out. You don't want to ruin the surprise."

He did, and we began chatting about his expanded responsibilities during the time Josie and I would be on vacation. A few minutes later, the door to exam room two opened, and Titan led the way out closely followed by Josie and Rooster.

"That was fast," I said, glancing down at the bandage on Titan's front paw.

"It was one of those carpet tacks," Josie said. "It was wedged in there pretty good."

"I just had some carpeting redone, and one of the workers must have dropped it," Rooster said.

"You might want to run the vacuum a couple of times to make sure there aren't any more buried in the rug," Josie said.

"Just as soon as I get home," Rooster said.

"He let you work on him?" I said.

"He was very good," Josie said. "We gave him a little shot to numb the area, and he settled right down. He's a tough guy."

"He gets that from his father," Rooster said.

"Hey, Rooster," I said. "Did I see you driving around with your ex-wife yesterday?"

"Yup. You probably did."

"Any juicy details you feel like sharing?" I said, grinning at him.

"Nope."

"Subtle," Josie said, shaking her head at me.

"It was worth a shot," I said. "How long is she staying in town?"

"She left this morning," he said. "I doubt if she'll be coming back anytime soon."

"Did you ever find out if she and your brother had something going on?" I said.

"She said no. And for the sake of my own peace of mind, I chose to believe her," he said, giving me a look that said *end of discussion*. "Thanks, Josie. Good job."

"No problem, Rooster. Just try to keep him from chewing the bandage. In a couple of days, he'll be good as new."

Rooster waved goodbye and headed for the door. Before he could open it, someone on the other side entered and stood in the doorway. He glanced at Rooster, then down at Titan who was already beginning to sniff the air and stepped to one side as they walked past. Rooster nodded at him on his way out.

"My, but he certainly is a colorful character," the man said as he removed his coat and hat. "Hello, ladies. What a lovely day."

"Hi, Jerome," I said. "I'm glad you're here. We're running low on a few things, and I was actually going to give you a call."

Jerome was the sales rep we used almost exclusively. He represented several different companies and carried a wide variety of items we used at the Inn. His prices were a bit high, but Josie and I had decided that one conversation with Jerome was a lot more efficient that us having to have a dozen different ones. As such, we were happy to pay a little extra for the convenience. Jerome was also a major source of information about what was happening in the dog world and loved to gossip.

"I'm a couple days early, but I'm going on vacation and trying to get everything ordered and processed before I go," he said.

"Where are you going?" Josie said.

"Cozumel. I can't wait."

"I've always wanted to go to Cozumel," Josie said. "I'd love to see the Mayan Ruins there. Are you going to check them out?"

"Josie, darling," he said, waving the idea off. "Do I look like the sort of man who would spend all day hiking through the wilderness just to climb a stack of old rocks?"

"Silly me," Josie said, laughing.

"Right after I land, I'll be checking in at the resort and heading to the pool to find the bucket of margaritas with my name on it."

We headed to my office and got settled in.

"I hear your dog show was a huge success," Jerome said, accepting the bag of bite-sized Snickers from Josie.

Remembering my promise to do a test run with my bathing suit in the mirror later on, I waved the bag away.

"Who'd you hear that from?" I said.

"Everyone," he said, popping one of the bite-sized into his mouth. "Of course, Fetch and Tug would have been happier if the Chesapeake had won Best in Group, but you can't win them all, right?"

"The Springer that won is a beautiful dog," I said.

"Yes, and it was the last dog that Alexandra Vincent ever judged," Jerome said, grabbing another of the bite-sized. "Dreadful news about her and her husband."

"That reminds me," I said to Josie. "We need to mail Alexandra's bag to her sister."

"What a way to go," Jerome said, frowning. "But at least it was probably quick, huh?"

"Yes, it probably was," Josie whispered.

"I met her a few times," he said. "She seemed to be a very sweet woman."

"She was," I said, nodding. "Let me ask you something, Jerome."

"Go right ahead," he said, smiling. "Apart from getting my hands on a big chunk of your hard-earned money, isn't that why I'm here?"

"We've always appreciated your brutal honesty, Jerome," Josie said, laughing.

"It is one of my better qualities, wouldn't you say?"

"Have you heard anything through the grapevine about a robbery at a clinic that specializes in dog semen?" I said.

"As a matter of fact I have," he said. "Apparently, there are some strong rumors that the people behind the robbery are very well-placed in the show dog world."

"Really?" I said. "Have any specific names come up?"

"No, not yet," he said, shaking his head. "But it can't be a very long list of potential suspects. Frozen samples from some of the top show dogs are worth a small fortune. As you know, the black market for dogs is big business and getting bigger. Say, how are those tracking devices working out?"

"The device needs some work before it's ready for primetime," Josie said. "The signal and the battery both need a serious upgrade."

"That seems to be the prevailing opinion. I heard the CEO of that company had an accident," he said. "He jumped off a fiord in

Norway wearing a bat suit. Those adventure types are definitely people to avoid. As I always say, you'll never be prone to injury when you're prone." He chuckled at his own joke. "He was lucky to get off with just two broken ankles."

"You are in the loop, aren't you?" I said.

"Of course," he said, reaching for another bite-sized and glancing at Josie. "Three's my limit. Don't let me have any more." He looked back at me. "And if I weren't in the loop, I'd just be one more guy pushing product, right?"

"What have you heard about Fetch and Tug lately?" I said.

"It's been pretty quiet the last couple of weeks, but thanks for reminding me," he said, reaching into his bag. "This is just a miniature sample, but the all the new marketing materials will be available for order in a couple of days."

He placed a small cardboard cutout on the desk. On it was the Fetch and Tug logo along with an action shot of Glen and Abby Wilson's Chesapeake Bay retriever.

"It is a great looking dog," he said. "But I probably would have stayed with Alexandra's Goldens."

"Wow, that was fast," I said, glancing at Josie. "I can't believe they're already in production."

"Why not?" Jerome said, frowning.

"Because the deal just got closed the other day," I said.

"What are you talking about? The deal closed last month."

Josie and I both sat upright.

"The deal closed last month?" I said.

221

"Yeah. I'm surprised you hadn't heard." He glanced back and forth at us and noticed our surprise. "What?"

"Nothing," I said. "It's just that we heard it hadn't closed yet."

"No, it was definitely wrapped up last month," he said. "And I got that from a very reputable source."

"Yeah, we thought we did as well," Josie said.

"I got it from one of their marketing VPs. Fetch and Tug thinks it's time to change breeds. Personally, I think they're going to regret dropping the Goldens, but it's their company, right? Okay, you guys ready to spend some money?"

We spent the next fifteen minutes placing our regular order and reviewing the new products he was now carrying.

"I've also got some great Christmas sweaters for dogs," he said, holding up a page from a catalog filled with photos of various breeds posing in hideous sweaters.

"Those poor dogs," I said, laughing. "The Doberman looks like he's saying kill me now."

"We're not really big on dog clothing, Jerome," Josie said, making a face.

"But I'm sure some of your customers are," he said, extending the catalog closer.

"Yeah, probably," I said. "But we really don't have room to display them in the reception area."

"Are you sure?" he said. "I thought that if you rearranged some of the furniture in the waiting room, you'd be able to fit in a nice display rack in the back corner."

Josie and I gave him a blank stare.

"Okay, you win," he said, laughing as he held up his hands in surrender. "Far be it for me to push."

"Have a great time in Cozumel, Jerome," I said, standing up.

"Oh, I will," he said, packing his bag. "I'll see you in a couple of weeks."

"Can't wait," Josie said.

Jerome smiled at both of us, then tossed the bag over his shoulder.

"Mayan Ruins," he said, shaking his head as he left the office.

I sat back down behind the desk, my mind racing.

"Questions?" Josie said, raising an eyebrow at me.

"Dozens."

Chapter 26

After Jerome had left, Josie was soon summoned to deal with another walk-in emergency, this one a Lab that had been chasing a tennis ball and scraped her side against a piece of rusted metal that was protruding from a backyard garden shed. The cut that ran along the Lab's ribcage was long, but fortunately, not deep, and Josie headed off leaving me alone in my office.

I started by scribbling down several questions that were rolling around in my head, then fired up my laptop. I began with a review of Fetch and Tug's website, then moved on to the various news articles about the robbery at the clinic. I took a short break and was staring out the window when an idea popped into my head that nagged at me and eventually turned into an earworm. But instead of a song that gets stuck in your head, this earworm couldn't carry a tune and just kept repeating *I wonder if* until I gave up and called Chief Abrams. Our conversation was short, and a fruitless, and incredibly depressing, half-hour followed when I reviewed all the stories about the hit and run that had killed Alexandra and her husband. I had just begun my search for the mailing address to send Alexandra's bag to when Josie returned and stretched out on the couch.

"How's the Lab doing?" I said, glancing up as I waited for the sister's website to load.

"She's sore, but she's going to be okay," Josie said as she made room for Captain on the couch. "Suzanne showed me a photo of the garden shed. One of the sides came loose and somehow got bent up at a ninety-degree angle. The dog could have easily gotten its throat slit. Not to mention one of her kids."

"How many stitches did she need?" I said.

"Just a few in a couple of spots," Josie said. "That's probably a lot less than her husband's going to need when he gets home tonight."

"Let me guess, it was on his list of things to do around the house, but he didn't get around to it," I said.

"Worse," Josie said. "He told her he'd already taken care of it."

"Uh-oh," I said. "Silly man."

"Did you find anything?" Josie said, pulling up a chair and sitting down next to me behind the desk.

"Not a lot that's new. But Jerome wasn't kidding about the Fetch and Tug deal. It's all over their website, and it made the news in at least two dog publications."

"Then why the heck didn't Alexandra know it was a done deal?" Josie said.

"I've been wondering the same thing. But do you remember when she was talking about her and husband's partnership?"

"Yeah. She handled the dogs, he handled all the business stuff."

"I guess it's not too much of a stretch to believe she might have been out of the loop," I said. "As long as she was left alone to do her thing with the dogs, maybe she was happy remaining oblivious to what was happening on the business side."

"But people must have been talking about it," Josie said. "At a minimum, she would have heard rumors, right?"

"I'm sure she did," I said. "But if her husband told Alexandra to do the usual, she might not have given it a second thought."

"The usual? You mean, like telling her to ignore the rumors, remind her that everyone else is jealous of their success, and saying: *You just need to trust me, Alexandra?*"

"Yeah, that usual," I said, nodding. "And they were married a long time. If her husband asked her to trust him, she probably did."

"Which brings us to the husband," Josie said. "Let me guess, you're thinking that Alexandra's husband might have been playing his own version of *Honey, I already fixed the garden shed.*"

"Yeah, I've been sitting here wondering why her husband needed to stay on the west coast to have a meeting with the Fetch and Tug people about their deal if the deal with the Wilson's Chesapeake had already closed a month earlier."

"And you've also been wondering why he didn't jump on the first plane as soon as he heard that someone had tried to kill his wife," Josie said.

"Yeah, it does makes me wonder," I said, nodding.

"Me too. Right from the start. You think the husband was up to a whole bunch of no-good, don't you?"

"I do. And I think I know the answer to why he didn't get on a plane."

"Oh, please, do tell."

"He didn't need to get on an airplane. He was already here."

"Now that could turn out to be a brilliant insight," Josie deadpanned. "Or one of the stupidest things you've ever come up with."

"Shut up," I said, laughing.

"Alexandra's husband as one of the dognappers?" she said, frowning. "I'm going to need a minute to process that."

"Take all the time you need," I said, studying the landing page of the sister's website.

"Why would the guy try to steal his own dogs?" Josie eventually said.

"It does seem odd, doesn't it?"

"I guess odd is a word for it. So, let's go with that," Josie said.

"Apart from unconditional love, what's the one thing that pair of Goldens brought Alexandra and her husband?"

"A ton of money," Josie said.

"Yes. And what is one of the first things people tend to do when they acquire something very valuable?"

Josie thought for a moment, then spread her arms in revelation.

"They insure it."

"Well done. You got it in one."

"You think this is an insurance scam?" Josie said, frowning.

"I think it might be part of it," I said. "I called Chief Abrams earlier, and he's doing a bit of checking at the moment."

"Okay, let's say I buy that possibility," Josie said. "What's the connection, if any, with the clinic that got robbed?"

"For the moment, I'm going to stick with money as the motive," I said.

"Alexandra's husband was planning on getting into the Black Market for dogs?"

We looked up when we heard a knock on the door and Chief Abrams poked his head in.

"Come on in, Chief," I said. "We're just sitting here kicking around some ideas."

"You know, putting our brains together and seeing if anything pops out," Josie said.

"I thought I smelled something," he said, sitting down on the couch. "Well, you were right."

"I knew it," I said. "They had a life insurance policy on the dogs, didn't they?"

"They certainly did. A big one."

"How big?" I said.

"A million per dog."

"Two million dollars?" Josie said. "Geez, that's a big policy to have on a couple of dogs."

"Not when you think about how much revenue those dogs have been bringing in the past few years," Chief Abrams said. "And if you're willing to pay the premium, there are companies out there that will underwrite just about anything."

"How did you find out about the policy?" Josie said.

"I called a friend at the FBI who handles insurance fraud," he said, shrugging. "It didn't take him long to find it."

"Was the FBI already suspicious?" I said, casually reviewing the sister's website.

"They weren't until I called," he said, chuckling. "Now, I'm pretty sure it's on their radar."

"Since their deaths were called a hit and run accident, nobody had any reason to ask a ton of questions, right?" I said, clicking on another page.

"Exactly. I also managed to have my buddy do a little digging into that clinic that got robbed."

"And?" I said, pausing my website search to look up at him.

"And for a company dealing with frozen dog semen, a substance not very high on the list of items law enforcement pays much attention to, they sure went to a lot of trouble to make sure nobody knew who owned it. It looks like the owners set it up using a spider web of shell companies somewhere in the Caribbean. It'll take the Feebs a few days to get a handle on it, but they'll figure it out."

"Would I be right if I was willing to bet that the clinic also had a sizeable insurance policy in place?" I said.

"You would. Well done," Chief Abrams said.

"Thanks," I said, flashing him a quick smile. "And the policy was written in a way that placed a value on each frozen specimen."

"It was. Most had a quoted market value somewhere between a thousand and twenty-five hundred bucks. But some of them were a lot higher. And a couple thousand specimens were stolen."

"The FBI found all this out in a couple of hours?" Josie said.

"I doubt if it took them that long," Chief Abrams said. "They probably found it while I was on hold."

"How can they figure all of that out so fast?" Josie said.

"Do you really want to know?" Chief Abrams said.

"Probably not," Josie said, shaking her head.

"Good call."

"So, not only do the thieves get to use the specimens for breeding, but the clinic owners also collect a very nice insurance settlement," I said. "That's a sweet deal, especially if the thieves and the owners are the same people."

"Have you been reading my notes?" Chief Abrams said, laughing.

"I'm sure a lot of the top breeders were storing specimens at that clinic," I said.

"You're thinking what, black market dogs?" Chief Abrams said.

"High-end designer dogs," Josie said. "They're usually bought by people with more money than they know what to do with."

"And in some countries, they're a real status symbol," I said. "A couple years ago, a Tibetan Mastiff puppy sold for almost two million bucks in China."

"You're joking, right?" Chief Abrams said.

We both shook our heads at him.

"Unbelievable. But you guys would know more about that world than I would," he said, shrugging. "So, we like the husband for being the so-called brains behind all of this, right?"

We both nodded.

"Including the part where Chef Claire's dogs got stolen?" he said.

"Yeah," I said.

"But Rooster's cousin, Coke Bottle, said he thought that the two people in the hunting camp sounded like they were a couple," Chief Abrams said.

"He did," I said.

"Okay, and since Alexandra's husband was with her when they got run over the other day, it sure would be nice to know who the mystery woman was in the hunting camp."

"It would," I said, nodding.

"You think she could be the one who did the hit and run?" Josie said.

"Well, I'm not sure," Chief Abrams said. "But I always like to keep things as simple as possible and start from what I do know and see where that takes me. And since we know the husband and that woman were working together, that's where I'd start."

"I guess that makes sense," Josie said, shrugging.

"You got any ideas, Detective Snoop?" Chief Abrams said.

"Despite your use of that rather disparaging nickname, as a matter of fact, I do," I said, making a face at him.

"And?"

"I suggest we start with her," I said, pointing at a photo of Alexandra's sister prominently displayed on her website.

"I can definitely see the family resemblance," Chief Abrams said.

"Well, we were going to mail her the bag that Alexandra forgot to take, but I think that I might drive up to her farm tomorrow and personally deliver it. And, of course, offer my deepest condolences for her loss while I'm there."

"I can't go anywhere tomorrow," Josie said. "I'm booked solid."

"That's okay," I said. "I don't mind going alone."

"There's no way you're going alone, Suzy," Chief Abrams said. "That woman might have just killed two people. Two people who were close family members, by the way. If she is involved, I doubt she'd worry too much about killing a complete stranger."

"Chief, is that your way of saying you'd love to go for a drive in my new SUV?" I said, smiling at him.

"No, that's my way of saying there's no way you're going alone. If anything happened to you, your mother would kill me."

Josie nodded.

"Not to mention what she'd do to Suzy."

Chapter 27

I pulled out of the driveway at seven and headed for the police station to pick up Chief Abrams. I found him standing outside the front door chatting with my mother. I pulled into an empty parking spot, put the car in park, and left it running. My mother immediately wandered over in my direction. I lowered the window and prepared myself for the worst.

"Hello, darling," she said, sticking her head through the window to give me a peck on the cheek.

"Good morning, Mom. What are you doing up and about so early?"

"Just checking to see how things are going," she said, smiling and nodding as she surveyed the SUV.

"How it's going in town, or with me?"

"Yes, darling," she said, beaming at me then glancing around the interior of the vehicle. "This is very nice. You did well."

"Thanks. And I got three grand off sticker."

"I heard. I knew you had it in you," she said. "Thank you, darling."

"For what?" I said, frowning.

"For doing something nice for me," she said, giving me a small smile.

"That was it? Buying a new car was the nice thing you wanted me to do for you?"

"Of course. Now I don't have to worry about you driving around in that old rust bucket."

"You're unbelievable."

"Yes, darling. And you overthink everything. So let's call it even. If you would just do what I ask the first time, life would be so much easier."

"I thought nagging me was the thing that kept you young," I said, glancing over as Chief Abrams climbed in the passenger seat.

"Speaking of nagging," she said, folding her arms across her chest.

"I made the call, Mom."

"Good girl. Now, you be careful today. And if anything does happen I expect you to get out of the way and let Chief Abrams handle it."

"Got it, Mom."

She locked eyes with me to emphasize her point, then leaned in and gave me another kiss on the cheek.

"Drive safe," she said. "And I'm making reservations for eight o'clock tonight at C's. Try not to be late. We need to review our itinerary for Grand Cayman."

"Itinerary? Geez, Mom, it's supposed to be a vacation," I said, shaking my head.

"What did I just say about listening to me the first time I asked you to do something?"

"Yeah, I heard," I said, putting the SUV in reverse. "But I must say, Mom, you're looking younger every day."

"Funny, darling."

"Yeah, I kinda liked that one myself," I said, giving her a goodbye wave.

I checked the rear view mirror, then backed out of the parking spot.

"She keeps you on your toes, doesn't she?" Chief Abrams said.

"Are you referring to you or me?" I said.

"Yeah," he said, laughing. "What are you doing?"

I kept glancing down at the navigation system as I slowly drove up Main Street.

"Trying to remember how to work this GPS thingy."

"GPS? We don't need no stinkin' GPS," Chief Abrams said with a fake accent.

"That was pretty good, Chief. The Treasure of the Sierra Madre, right?"

"That's the one," he said, nodding. "Just take 81 south, catch the Thruway east, then head north on 87 when we hit Albany. We should be there in about four hours."

"But we'll still need to find the sister's farm when we get there," I said.

"And if we can't find it, we'll turn on the GPS thingy. How about some music?"

"Sure," I said, glancing at the radio that had more buttons on it than the navigation system. "What do you like? No, let me guess. You're a country and western guy."

"Nope."

"Classical."

"No, I'm a jazz guy."

"You mean like Kenny G?"

He made a face at me I didn't know he had in his repertoire.

"No, I don't mean like Kenny G," he said. "I'm talking about Coltrane. Miles Davis."

"I think I might have heard the names," I said, frowning.

"Philistine."

He pulled a CD from his bag and inserted it into the player. A quiet piano riff began that was soon followed by a soft trumpet that effortlessly sat on top.

"Nice," I said.

"It's *Kind of Blue*. 1959.

"Good driving music."

"It's good for anything music," he said, adjusting his seat back. "How do you want to play it today?"

"I thought we'd just start by chatting with her and see how things go," I said, trying to tap the steering wheel along with the music.

"Have a chat with her, huh?" he said, laughing. "So, you don't really have a plan."

"No," I said, glancing over at him. "Once we get past the chatting stage, I don't have a clue. I figured we'd just improvise from there."

"So it's a jazz plan," he said, resting his head back and closing his eyes.

"There you go," I said, grinning. "Just call me The Jazz Detective."

"Well, anything's better than Detective Snoop."

"This music is really hard to keep time with," I said, abandoning my attempt at steering wheel percussion.

"Of course it's hard. It's Miles Davis."

"I like it, but I'm having trouble following the thread. Or figure out where it's going. You know what I mean?"

"Yeah," he said, opening his eyes and glancing over. "I could probably ballpark it."

"Funny. Have you spent much time in Saratoga Springs?" I said.

"A bit. I know some of the local cops."

"You sure do know a lot of people, Chief."

"I spent over twenty years with the state police. I know a lot of people everywhere," he said, reclosing his eyes. "Saratoga is a nice town. And I've been to the racetrack a couple of times. They love horses there like you love your dogs."

"So I've heard," I said, finally connecting with the melody. "This is really good."

"I'm glad you like it," he said. "If the sister gets twitchy at some point, let me handle it okay?"

"Of course."

"I called the chief of police last night and told him we were coming," Chief Abrams said.

"Won't that spook her off if she sees the cops hanging around?"

"I asked him to be present on the scene, but invisible," he said, glancing over at me. "He promised to keep his guys out of sight until I text him."

"Good. Thanks."

"You're convinced it's her, aren't you?"

"I am," I said, nodding. "It has to be her."

"Weird."

"Yeah. That's the word. You want to get lunch first?"

"That's probably not a bad idea," he said. "If things get squirrely, we might not get a chance to eat. Did you know the potato chip and the Club sandwich were supposed to have been invented in Saratoga?"

"I did not. But that sounds pretty good. When in Rome, right?"

"I thought we were going to Saratoga," he deadpanned.

"You're on your game today, Chief."

"It's the music," he said, reaching over to turn the volume up.

Apart from the music, we drove in silence for the next two hours. Chief changed CDs twice more, and I made a mental note to ask him to write down some suggestions of jazz classics for me to pick up. I wasn't sure if the music would become my go-to driving music, but I had a good idea it would be perfect for late nights in front of the fire when I had a glass of wine in my hand and way too much going on inside my head.

By the time we turned off Interstate 87 and saw the signs for Saratoga, I was relaxed, had a game plan formulated in my head and my game face on. We agreed to skip lunch, and I drove past a wooden white horse fence and turned into a long stretch of driveway that led up the hill to where the house and two large barns sat nestled among a stand of oak and maple trees.

I reached into the back seat and grabbed Alexandra's bag, then we hopped out of the car and took some time to stretch. I glanced around at the empty paddocks and felt the stiff breeze coming from the north.

"The horses must all be inside," I said.

"Smart horses," Chief Abrams said, zipping up his jacket. "It's cold."

I looked at the house and noticed a woman in the large fenced backyard tossing a tennis ball for two Golden Retrievers. Her back was to us and didn't see us heading her way. But the dogs noticed, and they forgot all about the tennis ball and galloped toward us and waited on the other side of the gate wagging their tails.

"Hey, Lucky. Lucy," I said. "How are you guys doing?"

"Gorgeous dogs," Chief Abrams said.

Both dogs stood on their hind legs and put their front paws on the top rail of the fence. I used both hands to rub their heads, then looked at the woman who was standing a few feet behind the dogs.

"Can I help you?" she said, glancing back and forth at us.

"We're sorry to just pop in on you, but I wanted to return Alexandra's bag," I said, extending the bag over the fence. "Sorry about the chewed strap. One of our Goldens got a bit carried away."

"Yes, I can see that," she said, glancing at the bag before refocusing on us. "Who are you?"

"I'm Suzy Chandler. And this is Chief Abrams."

"The police?" she said, raising an eyebrow.

"I'm just Suzy's traveling companion today," Chief Abrams said. "I'm the chief of police for Clay Bay. And way out of my jurisdiction if you're worried about that."

"No," she said, relaxing a bit. "Not worried, just curious."

"Are you Abigail Johnson?" I said.

"I am."

"I'm so sorry about Alexandra and her husband," I said. "She stayed with us recently when she judged our dog show."

"Oh, of course. And that's why you know the dogs," she said, opening the gate for us. "Alexandra mentioned you when she was here last week."

"Did she tell you what happened?" I said, stepping into the backyard.

"She did. Someone tried to steal Lucky and Lucy, and then tried to kill her," she said, tearing up.

I studied the pain on her face, then compared her appearance with Alexandra. They were about the same height, but Abigail was a bit heavier. And her hair was different. Where Alexandra had chosen to let her hair grow and stay gray, Abigail opted for short and a blonde rinse. She also wore glasses with round frames that reminded me of our local librarian. But the smile, although tight and probably forced, was identical to her sister's.

"Where did you find the dogs?" I said, kneeling down to pet both of them.

"Just after the accident, the police found them wandering around in an alley behind the hotel. My number was listed as one of the emergency contacts, so they called me. I drove to Boston and picked them up the other day."

"You're going to keep them?" I said.

"Of course," she said, smiling down at them. "Alexandra had me listed in the will as their appointed guardian. And they're the only thing left to keep her memory alive."

I thought about my rust bucket SUV now safely parked in Rooster's garage.

"Yeah, I get that. They seem happy here," I said, glancing around the large property. "But it must be a lot of work. Dogs and all those horses."

"The horses are all gone," she whispered. "I'm selling the farm, and the last of the horses were picked up yesterday."

"Why are you selling? It's a beautiful place," I said.

"I just can't deal with it anymore," she said, wiping her eyes. "Since the accident, I've been taking stock of my life. And I think it's time for a change."

"Where do you plan on going?" I said.

"Someplace warm," she said. "But not too warm for the dogs. I've been wracking my brain, but it's not that easy to find a place like that. Any suggestions?"

"Northern California would probably work," I said, giving it some serious thought. "Or maybe Hawaii."

She nodded and panned the horizon of the property.

"Can I ask you a question, Abigail?" I said.

"I guess. You've come a long way, so I the least I can do is answer a question," she said, shrugging.

"Do you have any idea who might have killed them?"

She exhaled audibly and fought back another round of tears.

"I have my ideas," she said. "I could never prove it, but, when you boil it all down, the dog business is what killed my sister and her husband."

"I'm not really following that thread, Abigail," I said.

"All that success, but it was never enough," she said. "Everybody always wanted more. In the end, does it really matter who was driving that car?"

"Actually, I think it does matter, Abigail," I said. "At a minimum, it matters from a justice standpoint."

242

"Justice?" she said, scuffing the brown grass with the tip of her boot. "Will dispensing justice bring them back?"

"No, it won't," I said. "Nothing is going to do that."

"Then it sounds like justice falls into the same category of other things that won't bring them back. Right next to sympathy, grief, and fond memories."

"It's hard to argue with that," I said.

"Yes, it is," she said, staring at me.

She exhaled again, wiped her eyes, and draped Alexandra's bag over her shoulder.

"Thank you for bringing the bag," she said. "But if you'll excuse me, I need to get ready for a meeting with my realtor."

"Of course," I said.

"It was nice meeting you, Suzy. Alexandra had some wonderful things to say about you and your partner. What was her name?"

"Josie."

"Yes, Josie. The beauty queen vet," she said. "Chief Abrams, it was very nice meeting you as well."

"The pleasure was all mine," he said. "Good luck wherever you end up."

"One can only hope," she said, giving us a small wave and turning her back as she began to stroll back toward the house.

"Take care of yourself," I said. "Alexandra."

Alexandra froze in her tracks, then turned and stared at me.

"When did you know?" she said, continuing to stare at me in disbelief.

"I've had a pretty good idea since I learned the Fetch and Tug deal closed over a month ago," I said. "But I wasn't convinced until I saw the thermal underwear poking out your sleeve. It's actually a clever way to look heavier than you are. Are you wearing two pairs?"

"Three," she whispered.

"I think I understand the financial pressure your husband's business decisions put you in, but how does a woman who is as genuinely nice, as sweet as you are, have the ability to run two people down like that?"

Alexandra casually reached behind her back. I doubted if it was to scratch an itch. Chief Abrams noticed it as well.

"Don't make things worse, Alexandra," he said, drawing his gun.

She held up both hands, and Chief Abrams approached her and removed the gun. He entered a text message into his phone and moments later, four policemen approached from different directions carrying rifles.

"To answer your question, Suzy," Alexandra said. "What I experienced that night was what I believe psychiatrists call an episode of sub-psychotic rage. And I have to say that it was oddly pleasurable."

"You'll excuse me if I can't quite get my head around that idea, Alexandra," I said.

"I wouldn't expect you to understand it. You've never had family members do anything close to what those two did to me."

"You're right. I haven't. You knew your husband and your sister were the ones behind the botched dognapping."

"Of course," she said, nodding. "It was part of our plan."

"Why would you use those two idiots to steal the dogs? Couldn't you have just hidden them on your own?""

"That was my husband's idea. He wanted a third-party involved that could be blamed. And those two were the perfect idiots. Apart from the stealing the wrong dogs of course."

"You were going to steal them, relocate them to a safe place, maybe here, and then report them missing and collect on the insurance policy."

"Yes, all the endorsement money was drying up, and it was time to retire Lucky and Lucy as show dogs. As you've obviously figured out, my husband's business skills were somewhat lacking. By the time I realized that we were already incredibly overextended."

The policemen reached the four corners of the fence, and the dogs barked then trotted off to greet them. Chief Abrams held a hand up asking them to wait. The cops rested their rifles on the fence railing and said hello to the dogs while keeping a close eye on what was happening inside the fence.

"And your sister?" I said.

"Abigail was also in serious debt," Alexandra said. "She came to us to ask for a loan to keep the horse farm afloat, and we explained to her our own situation. Then we started talking and came up with a plan that was going to solve all our problems."

Alexandra let loose with a crazy cackle.

"Then your husband and sister started sleeping together," I said.

"At some point, yes," she said, tearing up again.

"But everything changed with your partnership when they tried to drop that box on you the day of the dog show, right?"

"It did."

"And you were the one who warned them not to try to steal the dogs from the Inn that night weren't you?"

"I was."

"I knew they were in that storage area," I whispered.

"What?"

"Nothing," I said, refocusing. "You couldn't take the risk of them getting arrested."

"No. After it had become clear they planned to kill me, I decided that it would be better to postpone stealing Lucky and Lucy. If they had been arrested, I was worried about what they might tell the police. They probably had a cover story blaming me for all of it."

"So you just decided to wait a week," I said.

"Yes, I did."

"And that's why you didn't feel the need to hire any security to protect you," I said.

"You don't forget a thing, do you, Suzy?"

"I have my moments. You knew their next attempt wouldn't happen until the next show."

"I wasn't sure, but I figured they would want to talk with me first. You know, try to convince me the box falling was an accident, get me to relax and drop my guard before they tried again."

"The three of you met at the hotel in Boston, then they headed off to have dinner."

"Yes, we had an argument, and I told them I had to prepare for the dog show and stormed out of the room in a huff. Then I went straight to my rental car and...well, you know the rest."

"But not before you switched wallets with your sister," I said.

"Of course," she said. "And not before I also called to report my rental car as stolen."

"It was a very good plan," I said. "I'm impressed."

"That's what I thought," she said. "And apart from some pointed questions from the insurance companies, nobody has batted an eye. Except for you, of course. I'm the one who should be impressed, Suzy."

"Thanks. It's kind of a hobby."

Chief Abrams snorted.

"The owner of the specimen clinic that was robbed is listed as AHA Industries," Chief Abrams said.

"How on earth did you find that out?" she said, baffled.

"I've got friends in the FBI," he said. "It took a while. Eventually, they tracked it down in the Cayman Islands."

"Yes, we were vacationing down there a few years ago, and it seemed like the perfect place to register the company. The people down there were most accommodating. For the right price, of course."

"I'm going down there in a couple of weeks on vacation," I said.

"You'll love it," Alexandra said. "It's gorgeous."

"I'm sure I'll burn," I said. "I don't tan, I stroke."

"You'll excuse me if I don't have much sympathy for your vacation sunburn, Suzy."

"Sure, sure. AHA Industries is an acronym, isn't it? Alexandra, Harold, and Abigail."

"Yes."

"And the clinic?" I said, sending a text message of my own.

"What about it?" Alexandra said.

"You were stealing show dogs and getting samples from the males then breeding them with the females?"

"Yes, it was an elaborate scheme my husband came up with. I hated the idea, but we were in so much trouble financially. We didn't do a lot of breeding, though. It was primarily done so we could build the semen inventory as quickly as possible."

"The policy was written to cover individual samples so the bigger the inventory, the bigger the payout," I said.

"It added up in a hurry," she said, beaten.

"How much were you going to walk away with?" Chief Abrams said.

"Between the insurance policy on Lucky and Lucy and the clinic, about four million," she said, shrugging.

"I guess stealing from yourself is a lot easier than robbing other people," he said.

"I'm no longer quite so sure about that, Chief Abrams."

"Where are all the dogs you stole?" I said.

"They're at my daughter's place in the Adirondacks," she said.

"You got your daughter involved in all of this?" I said, staring at her.

"Yes, and my son as well."

"Geez, that's despicable, Alexandra," I said, my spirits dropping another couple of notches.

"You don't have to tell me that, Suzy. Things just started spiraling out of control."

"What a mess," I said. "And you're probably still trying to figure out you managed to end up in this spot."

"I am," she said, softly. "But I imagine I'll have lots of quiet time to figure it out."

"What about the life insurance on you and your husband?" he said.

"That was supposed to go to my children," she said, tears streaming down her cheeks. "But they won't be getting that now, will they?"

"I seriously doubt it, Alexandra," he said. "Maybe your husband's policy will pay off if you can spin a good enough story to the insurance company."

"Do your kids know you were the one who killed them?" I said.

"No. But I'm sure they will soon."

She sat down on the grass and started sobbing uncontrollably. Lucky and Lucy left the policemen and bounded toward her. They nuzzled her neck, and she wrapped her arms around them tightly.

I stared down at them and choked back the lump forming in my throat.

"There's no way out of this, is there?" she said, without looking up from the dogs.

"If this was just an insurance scam, you might get off a lot easier," Chief Abrams said. "But we're talking about a double murder here."

"They had it coming," she whispered.

"Keep telling yourself that," he said. "Maybe it will help you get through some of those long nights in prison."

A black SUV with tinted windows roared up the driveway. Everyone turned to look at it and soon Jessica Talbot and Jerry the Cameraman emerged from the vehicle.

"Is that the reporter who covered your dog show?" Alexandra said.

"That's her," I said, waving at Jessica.

"What the heck is she doing here?" Chief Abrams said.

"I called her," I said, shrugging.

"Why on earth did you do that?" he said, staring at me.

"Well, ever since we did everything we could to make her miserable the whole time she was in Clay Bay, I've needed to find a way to make it up to her. You know, try to do something nice for her."

"I get it," Chief Abrams said. "So, it's kind of a Karma thing, right?"

"No, actually, it's more of a mom thing."

Chapter 28

Chief Abrams nodded at the four policemen, and they came through the gate and surrounded Alexandra who was still hugging both of her Goldens. Seeming to sense the final goodbye nature of the interaction, the cops hung back and let the scene play itself out. Chief Abrams shook hands with one of the four then turned to me.

"Suzy, I'd like you to meet Chief Art Solomon," Chief Abrams said. "Art, this is Suzy."

We shook hands, and he studied my face.

"You're the one with all the dogs, right?" Chief Solomon said.

"Yeah, we have a bunch," I said, shrugging.

"We've got two at home," he said. "A poodle and a Doberman. That's more than enough. How do you find the time to solve crimes?"

"I manage somehow," I said. "And I think I might be a bit obsessed."

"So I hear," he said, smiling.

"Have you been talking to my mother?" I said. "Look, I need to go speak with the woman heading our way, then I was wondering if you could give her a few minutes with Alexandra before you take her away?"

252

The two chiefs glanced at each other before Chief Solomon nodded his okay. I headed down the driveway to meet Jessica and Jerry.

"Hi, folks," I said. "Thanks for coming. How are you, Jessica?"

"Hello, Suzy," Jessica said, giving me a cold stare. "Why am I here?"

"Because of Alexandra Vincent," I said. "Hi, Jerry."

"Hey, Suzy," he said, smiling.

"Alexandra Vincent?" Jessica said, frowning. "The woman who judged the dog show?"

"Yes."

"You dragged me out here to do another dog story?" Jessica said. "What on earth is the matter with you?"

"There are a lot of theories floating around about that," I said. "But this isn't a dog story."

"Then what is it?" she snapped.

I took a few deep breaths and fought back the urge to punch her in the nose.

"If you can put your fangs away for a few minutes and just listen I think you'll understand."

Jessica nodded, and I started talking. When I finished recounting the Cliff Notes version five minutes later, she was not only listening intently but appeared to be salivating. I stopped talking and slid my hands into my jacket to keep them warm as

253

the wind whipped. Jessica's hair fluttered in the breeze, but it always seemed to settle back in place when the gusts subsided.

"How do you get your hair to do that?" I said, baffled.

"Do what?" Jessica said, even more baffled by my question.

"Never mind," I said. "So, do you think this is a story?"

"You're joking, right?" Jessica said, laughing. "This could win me a Pulitzer."

"I know you've been looking for human interest stories that might soften your reputation, and I thought you might be able to tell Alexandra's story from her perspective. A very nice person who feels trapped and ends up losing everything."

"So, now you're a producer as well?" Jessica said, going for incredulous but landing on smug.

I so wanted to smack her in the nose.

"No, I would never assume anything like that," I said. "It just seems like it has the potential to be a great human interest story."

"It has the potential to be a lot of stories," she said, glancing at Alexandra who was still hugging her dogs tight. "Can I ask you something?"

"Sure."

"Why did you call me with it? Every journalist on the planet would kill for this story."

I scuffed the driveway with the tip of my shoe.

"My mother kind of made me do it," I said, embarrassed.

"Your mother? How quaint," Jessica said, laughing.

"Yeah, I figured that was the reaction you'd have," I said. "It's complicated."

"Oh, please, do tell," she said, almost taunting me.

"Well, my mother taught me that it's always better to have somebody who owes you a favor than it is to make them an enemy with revenge on their mind."

"And you think that I'm now going to owe you a favor?"

"No, I'll be more than happy to call this one a draw, Jessica. I heard that the network executives still weren't sure about bringing you to New York. And I thought this might help."

Jessica stared at me like I was a creature from outer space.

"You have to be the strangest woman I've ever met," she said, eventually.

"Yeah, I get that a lot. So what do you say?"

"I say I'm in," she said, turning all business. "Jerry, get some panoramic shots of the property while I go talk with the woman. When you're done, join me. We'll probably have to do most of the interviews from prison, but that should work really well with the new show concept."

"Got it," Jerry said, lifting the camera to his shoulder.

"Did you hear that information from Bob?" she said, refocusing on me.

"Indirectly, yes."

"Bob. What a piece of work," she said, shaking her head. "He always tried so hard to give me what I wanted."

"You and Bob are no longer an item?"

"No," she whispered. "He broke it off."

"Bob broke up with you?" I said, stunned.

"Yes. Apparently, his heart belongs to someone else," she said, laughing. "I told him not to worry about a minor detail like that, and that we could still have a lot of fun. But it turns out that Bob is a traditionalist."

"Who's the woman?"

"He wouldn't tell me," Jessica said. "It doesn't matter. Apart from being on the other side of the breakup for the first time ever, I'm going to be just fine."

"I have no doubt, Jessica."

I made a mental note to have a conversation with my mother.

"I'm moving to New York in a couple of weeks," she said. "And this is the perfect story for my first show."

"Congratulations. I guess you were finally able to convince them you could pull off warm and fuzzy, right?"

"No, I finally convinced them to drop all of that nonsense. I told senior management that they should be going the other way with me," she said, smiling. "You know, play to my strengths, and not trying to minimize them."

"Dark, mean, and edgy?" I said, raising an eyebrow.

"Yeah," she said, nodding. "Close enough."

"So, no morning show for the masses?"

"Absolutely not. A weekly primetime show called *The Evil Lurking in Us All*. And this story is perfect. Thanks for bringing it to me. Although it's probably not going to play out the way you were thinking."

"Yeah, probably not," I said. "But try to do me a favor, Jessica."

"We're back to that now, huh?" she said, laughing. "What do you think I owe you, Suzy?"

"Just try not to make Alexandra out to be too much of a monster."

She thought about it, then nodded.

"Okay. I'll see what I can do. Nice seeing you, Suzy."

"The pleasure was all mine, Jessica."

She waved, and I watched her stroll toward Alexandra. I watched as they began to chat, and laughed when the Goldens jumped up to say hello and Jessica let loose with a howl. Jerry the Cameraman walked up next to me and shook his head when he saw Jessica's reaction to the dogs.

"She really is a piece of work," he said, staring at Jessica.

"Are you going to miss her after she's gone?"

"I'm going to New York with her," Jerry said.

"What?"

"Yeah, I managed to weasel my way into a producer role on her new show."

"How the heck did you do that?"

"With a few carefully worded comments about a particular piece of footage from a dog show," he said, grinning at me.

"We deleted all of that," I said, frowning. "And I made Josie swear that she didn't send you a copy."

"Yeah, but Jessica doesn't know that," he said, laughing.

"You blackmailed her?"

"Blackmail is such an ugly word."

"Are all the people in your industry like the two of you?"

"No, most of them are very nice," he said. "And please don't lump me in with her. Jessica's in a class by herself."

"But why would you want to keep working with her?" I said, frowning.

"Because she's a rising star. And the chance to hitch your wagon to one of those doesn't come along very often," he said, shrugging.

"Opportunity trumps integrity?"

"Hey, I gotta eat, too."

With my contempt for the human race at an all-time high, I followed him as he headed for the backyard. I walked toward Alexandra to say goodbye. When she saw me coming, she excused herself from Jessica and met me near the gate.

"Thank you, Suzy," Alexandra said.

"For what?"

"For giving me the opportunity to tell my side of the story somewhere other than in the courtroom."

"Don't mention it," I said. "I hope it helps."

"We'll see," she said, glancing at Jessica. "But I'm going to have to stay on my toes. That woman is a snake."

"Well, at least you know what species you're dealing with going into it," I said.

"Can I ask you to do something for me?" Alexandra said, her eyes pleading.

"Why not?" I said, shrugging. "There seems to be a lot of that going around today."

"Would you be willing to take Lucky and Lucy with you? Keep them with you and Josie, or find them a good home?"

"I'd be honored, Alexandra."

Tears started rolling down her eyes then dried in the wind.

"Thank you. I'll go get them," she said, heading for the dogs.

Chief Abrams approached, and we both watched Alexandra hug her dogs again.

"She asked you to take the dogs, didn't she?" he said.

"Yeah. There were so many things floating around my head, I completely forgot about what would happen to the dogs."

"That's not like you," he said.

"No. I must be slipping."

"I'm sure you'll get it back," he said.

"It's so sad."

"It is. But at least you were able to give Jessica's career a boost," he deadpanned.

"Funny."

"I was going for ironic, but whatever," he said, draping an arm over my shoulder. "You did good, Suzy."

"Then why do I feel like crap?"

259

"Because people you thought you knew let you down again," he said, watching Alexandra as she headed for my SUV with both dogs trailing close behind. "I've been doing this stuff longer than I care to remember, and it happens all the time."

"How do you deal with it?" I said, glancing at him.

"I always try to follow a very simple rule."

"This oughta be good."

"When all else fails, lower your expectations."

I watched as Alexandra opened the door and the dogs effortlessly hopped up on the backseat. She gave them a final embrace, then slowly headed back toward us. She stopped to hug me, then approached the four cops who were waiting patiently in the backyard. Chief Abrams and I waved goodbye, then climbed in the SUV and spent a few minutes petting the dogs before I turned around and slowly drove down the driveway.

"You want to get something to eat before we head home?" Chief Abrams said.

"No, I don't have much of an appetite at the moment," I said.

"Yeah, I get that," he said, reaching into his bag. "Don't worry, it happens to all the great ones from time to time."

"You really should have gone into standup, Chief."

He popped *Kind of Blue* into the CD player and leaned back in his seat. The soft piano riff started, followed by the plaintive whisper of a trumpet that slowly began to swell. I stared out at the empty stretch of highway and noticed snowflakes drifting past as the car hit seventy.

"I'm feeling something different listening to it this time," I said.

"That's because your mood has changed," he said, his eyes closed.

"Interesting. Does that happen a lot when you listen to jazz?"

"Sometimes," he said, yawning. "But it always happens when I listen to Miles."

Epilogue

The events of our day in Saratoga Springs stayed with me, and my dominant mood seemed stuck somewhere between a muted sadness and a relentless indifference to most of the things happening in and around my world. Except for the dogs. My four-legged friends continued to provide joy and offer hope on a daily basis, and I was again struck by the notion of how much they could teach their human brethren if we'd only take the time to listen.

As much as we would have loved to keep Lucky and Lucy, the prospect of having six dogs in the house was a bit too much for even us to consider. And after several conversations with Josie and Chef Claire, we eventually decided to give them to a family that had a farm just outside of town, thereby disappointing a dozen other people who had immediately raised their hands when we first announced the two Goldens were available for adoption.

Chef Claire and I watched the family drive down the driveway with the dogs and two young kids crammed into the backseat, then headed to the living room where Al was terrorizing Captain. I sprawled out on the couch with Chloe and watched Al do everything he could to get the Newfie up off the floor.

"I ran into Rooster today," I said. "His cousin is going to get probation."

"He better hope I don't run into him again," Chef Claire said.

"He's Florida bound," I said. "I doubt if we'll be seeing him around here again."

Josie entered the living room wearing one of the micro-bikinis my mother had bought for all three of us.

"I don't care what your mother says or tries to do," Josie said. "I am not wearing this thing."

"Wow, that is small," Chef Claire said.

"I don't know whether to wear mine," I said. "Or floss my teeth with it."

"Any ideas?" Josie said, glancing back and forth at us.

I thought for a moment, then an evil grin appeared on my face.

"Go change," I said to Josie. "And bring all three bikinis with you when you come back out."

Josie shrugged, then headed off. A few minutes later she came back wearing sweats and a tee shirt holding all three of the suits. She handed them to me and stretched out on the floor next to Captain.

"What are you going to do? Throw them in the fireplace?" Chef Claire said.

"No, something better," I said. "Al. Come here, boy."

Al trotted over and grabbed all three bikinis out of my hand. He settled down behind the couch and started working his way through them. We all kept a close eye on him to make sure he chewed but didn't swallow.

"Gee, I'm sorry, Mrs. C.," Josie said, laughing. "But the dog ate my swimsuit."

"Exactly," I said. "We're probably sending Al a mixed message, but duty calls, right?"

"You're a genius," Chef Claire said.

"It's just part of the evil lurking inside us all," I said.

I flashed back on the first episode of Jessica's new show we'd watched last night. Despite a few times where I thought Jessica had gone too far, Alexandra came across as an orange-clad shell of a woman who'd been scorned, out of options, and increasingly desperate. I knew it probably wouldn't have any impact on the jury, but I felt a bit better knowing that the general public had an opportunity to hear the details directly from Alexandra. Jessica had come across as stern but capable, two qualities Josie found unusual for a reptile to possess, and I was sure the show would be a hit.

I reached for my wine and the printed itinerary my mother had put together for our trip. She'd put a lot of work into making sure we had a chance to experience some of her favorite things in Grand Cayman, so I had committed myself to being on my best behavior the entire week. My mother was still being tight-lipped about whether or not she was the mystery woman who'd stolen Bob's heart, and I had also committed myself to getting it out of her while we were on vacation.

I glanced behind the couch and laughed when I saw the purple and yellow string dangling from Al's mouth. He paused to look up at me, then went back to work.

"Good job, Al," Josie said. "Should we save the scraps to show your mother?"

"Great idea," I said. "Otherwise, she'd never believe us."

Chef Claire bent down and collected what was left of the bikinis. She then had a brief tug of war over the string Al was determined to polish off.

"That's enough, Al," Chef Claire said. "How about a cookie?"

Al dashed for the kitchen and waited for Chef Claire to deliver. She returned with the box and gave two to all four dogs. I stretched back out on the couch and gently stroked Chloe's head.

"What is this music?" Josie said, frowning.

"It's Miles Davis. *Kind of Blue*."

"Melancholy," she said, nodding.

"Good word."

Made in the USA
Las Vegas, NV
05 June 2021

24217481R00154